MW00931773

I SAID RUN: A PSYCHOLOGICAL THRILLER

BRITNEY KING

COPYRIGHT

Hot Banana Press

Cover Design by Britney King LLC

Cover Image by Britney King LLC

Copy Editing by Librum Artis

Proofread by Proofreading by the Page

First Edition: 2024

ISBN 13: 9798884660960

ISBN 10: 8884660960

britneyking.com

"A lie can travel half way around the world while the truth is putting on its shoes."

— **Mark Twain**

PROLOGUE

Eve's pounding heart sounds like a war drum as she dashes through the shadowy forest, weaving between skeletal trees and vaulting over fallen logs slick with moss. Malevolent shadows seem to grasp at her from all sides as enraged bellows ring out behind her, driving her forward on raw and blistered feet.

In her mind's eye, Eve pictures Scott's warm smile, a shard of hope guiding her home. She has no choice but to survive this nightmare, if only to get back to him. Scott needs to know that none of this horror is his fault. He is the reason she can't give up hope. God knows there have been times during her endless captivity in Jenkins's remote cabin that she nearly has. With each passing day trapped in that windowless prison, Jenkins has sadistically chipped away at her soul, twisting her into someone unrecognizable, even to herself.

Eve knows this is her last chance to break free. This morning, she had feigned sleep as Jenkins unlocked her handcuffs to take her to the bathroom. Before he could react, Eve had grabbed the vase by her bed —a cruel gift from Jenkins after his last violation — and smashed it over his head. This time, she will not be going back to that cabin, at least not alive.

Not that Jenkins is making escape easy. He knows the secrets of these woods far better than she does. He has been searching for her since dawn, using every twisted tactic to hunt her in this isolated wilderness. Eve feels as if she is running in circles, each mile through the shadowy woods only leading her back to that cabin and its unspeakable horrors.

Eve gasps. She can finally see a break in the oppressive trees. If she can just make it into the open, she might find help. Behind her, Jenkins's enraged shouting draws closer, like the icy breath of some lurking evil. Fear alone seems to propel her leaden legs faster, despite the pain. Her lungs burn like wildfire, but the path behind promises terrors far worse than any agony that might lie ahead. Freedom is within reach if she can just summon the strength.

With a final desperate burst, Eve breaks through the tree line and stumbles into the clearing, each breath she takes akin to inhaling fire. Her lungs are searing, but she can't stop. The open field ahead shines like a flare beneath the pale moonlight, beckoning her away from the menacing shadows of the woods. But as Eve runs, she can feel those same shadows watching, waiting to swallow her whole.

Jenkins's demented voice rings out an instant before he explodes from the woods behind her, his face twisted in fury. "There you are!"

Eve's legs course with mindless panic, each step a frantic plea for life as his taunting words echo in her ringing ears.

Rivulets of sweat pour down Eve's face, despite the icy winter air lashing her skin. Behind her, Jenkins's thundering footsteps only grow louder.

But ahead, about a hundred yards away, the safety of a country road waits—Eve's only hope. Calling on the last dregs of strength left in her broken body, Eve forces herself onward toward that thin chance of salvation.

Freedom is suddenly within her reach. She can see headlights slicing through the darkness. With a final burst, she sprints the last distance and collapses on the blessed asphalt, lungs heaving violently. But it isn't enough.

As the headlights fade into the distance, Eve watches her fleeting hope disappear with them. Still, she can't let Jenkins drag her back to that hellish cabin. Forcing herself up, Eve stumbles on just as the roar of another engine meets her ears. *A car is coming.*

Every muscle screaming, Eve lurches toward the approaching car like a woman possessed. She staggers out of the shadows, waving her arms and screaming for help. But the truck doesn't slow, its driver staring resolutely ahead, as if there is no desperate woman flailing by the roadside.

"Help me!" Eve cries again, but the taillights only shrink further into the distance as her chance at rescue accelerates down the road. Turning, Eve sees Jenkins, and knows her fate is sealed.

He stands mere feet away, chest heaving but grinning with sinister delight. Eve turns to run again, but her legs buckle beneath her. She can only watch helplessly as Jenkins closes the distance between them.

"Please..." Eve croaks, her throat ragged. "Don't do this..."

But her pleas go unheard. Jenkins's hulking shadow engulfs her as he leers. "No more running, sweetheart. Let's go home."

His powerful hands clamp around her arms like iron chains, wrenching her to her feet. In her mind's eye, Eve can already see the cruel games that await back at that godforsaken cabin, the twisted punishments Jenkins will gleefully devise for this escape attempt.

As he drags her weakened body toward the leering forest, Eve sobs, the reality of her grim future now agonizingly clear. She has seen it too many times before—in a few short hours, the others will feast on her insides, and whatever is left will join the rows of markers in Jenkins's immaculate garden.

Unless...

Eve's frantic gaze fixes on the worn hunting knife at Jenkins's hip, its handle smoothed by use. The polished steel glints in the moonlight like a beacon.

Letting her legs go limp, she forces Jenkins to take her dead weight as he hauls her along. His focus stays locked ahead. The knife waits just out of reach at his side, but if Eve moves fast enough...

Her heart slamming against her ribs, she makes her desperate play. With a burst of adrenaline, her hand shoots out and closes around the knife's grip. In one smooth motion, she rips it from the sheath.

Jenkins turns, his eyes widening with shock and rage. "You little—"

1

Four months earlier

Eve's gaze flits to the clock on the kitchen wall, its relentless ticking counting down the minutes of her life. Knife in hand, she slices vegetables by rote, imagining Scott's expression when he sees what she's been up to.

The pungent smell of onions waters her eyes, but even that can't wipe the smile from her face. Her mind replays the intimate moments from earlier— Scott's warm hands exploring her body, his lips against her neck as he murmured in her ear, making her giggle and melt into his embrace. She flushes thinking about his lips trailing down her skin, their bodies moving together in perfect sync. Those passionate memories dance in her mind, mingled with the sound of their hushed laughter echoing in her ears. Finally her thoughts come to rest on the thrilling ride on which she and Scott have embarked—a journey of burning desire that ignites a fire deep within, consuming her from the inside out.

"Remember when we talked about seeing the world?" Lucy's

voice crackles through the phone, thrusting Eve back through the years to carefree days spent poring over maps, eager fingers tracing imaginary routes, heart pumping with wanderlust. Now those far-flung dreams have faded into mortgage payments, grocery lists, and newlywed bliss. Her sister still clings to that restless spirit, refusing to be tied down, though Eve senses it isn't for lack of trying.

Lucy's voice reels Eve back from her reminiscing. "You there?"

The old-fashioned rotary phone fits the quaint charm of their place perfectly. Eve nods reflexively, looping the phone cord around her finger.

"I'm here," Eve says, releasing the cord and tucking back a loose strand of hair. "Just working on dinner."

Her eyes skim over the open cookbook, the words a mere backdrop to her churning thoughts. She flashes back to that tiny Moroccan joint they'd found, each bite a riot of flavor on her tongue. Longing stirs within, bittersweet and tangled up in memories of adventures past. With a sigh, Eve tries to focus on the task at hand.

"Like I was saying," Lucy huffs, her words dripping with exasperation and amusement, "you used to want to conquer the globe, and now I can't even get you to Hawaii, of all places..."

Eve's retort is quick. "I told you; I've got things here I need to handle."

"Things?" Lucy's laughter crackles down the line. "What, like watching paint dry?"

Eve flicks the cord over her shoulders and once again picks up the knife, tightening her grip on its steady weight. The cold steel is a familiar, comforting presence. "Just things."

"Oh, come on! I remember the Evie who would've hopped on a flight with nothing but a half-packed backpack. And maybe not even that..."

Eve's gaze flickers, nostalgia and defiance mingling. She can't deny that restless past still lurking beneath the surface. With a shrug, she manages, "Times change, Luc—people evolve."

"Yeah. Or maybe they just give up."

Lucy's prod hits its mark, stinging Eve's pride. Anger snaps her fraying patience. Her palm slaps the counter, sending plates wobbling dangerously. This is old ground they have covered countless times over the last few weeks, and Eve refuses to tread it again.

Her sister's sigh takes the hard edge off her tone. "Look, I didn't mean—"

"Mom always said you needed roots," Eve shoots back, bitterness carrying the weight of unspoken history. She hacks at the last of the bell peppers with controlled fury, venting her frustration. "Anyway, I've gotta run."

After Eve hangs up, her thoughts linger on her mother's meticulously tended garden, the way each plant had its designated place and purpose and considers planting one herself come spring. Stability has long been important in her family, the one principle they hold above all others. Her sister often accuses Eve of trading one cage for another, but Eve doesn't see it that way. Yet, as Scott's cheerful whistling and footsteps near from the direction of the hallway, her facade of a smile cracks beneath its weight. Lucy has gotten under her skin.

"Hey, gorgeous." Scott's greeting comes easily, his peck landing on her cheek. "Smells amazing in here."

Eve's answer is automatic, too rehearsed. "Thanks. Just messing around."

"Messing around, huh?" His raised brow speaks volumes, a gleam of playfulness in his eyes. "I like the sound of that."

As they sit down to eat, Eve struggles to suppress her uneasiness. Each bite tastes like sawdust, each swallow a battle against the constriction in her throat. Growing up, they always had a cook, and it was a skill she had never cared for nor needed to learn. Until now.

She stares out the window at the manicured lawns and identical houses and sighs, feeling the weight of their sameness pressing down on her. Only her sister can make her feel this way.

Scott's brow furrows with genuine concern, his voice gentle but persistent. "You sure everything's all right?"

"Of course," she lies, forcing a laugh. "I've just had this headache all day—I can't seem to shake it..."

His eyes say plenty—care and uncertainty mingling—but he lets it go, doesn't push further. The rest of the meal passes in silence. Eve finally breaks as she clears the plates.

"I got another call from Lucy," she says, her voice matter-of-fact. "She's hellbent on getting me to Maui."

"Your sister lives in a dream world."

"Totally delusional, right?"

He shrugs, as practical as ever. "I mean, maybe if we had the money, and maybe if there wasn't so much going on around here—"

Eve interjects, understanding the impracticality all too well. "No, I know—with the renovations and all, I told her it's not feasible. Not right now."

"Maybe next year..."

She nods. "We'll see."

A topic change can't divert the obvious. Scott knows Lucy's patterns. "Another breakup?"

Eve sighs again, her thoughts heavy as she confirms his insight. "Yep."

"Your sister never did fare very well alone."

Eve's voice carries a mix of empathy and frustration. "I know. But she sounded really low this time."

Scott offers a pragmatic fix. "You've got enough on your plate. Why doesn't she invite your parents out instead? Maybe you should reach out to them."

Eve had indeed made that call to her father, but it hadn't resulted in the support she'd hoped for. She'd hoped he might mention flying her out on one of the company jets or chartering her a plane, but he didn't.

Her grip on the conversation tightens, replaying her father's words in her mind. "'Sweetheart, if travel is what you wanted, you should have stayed single.'"

A fleeting thought had crossed her mind, unspoken, yet present. "Scott wouldn't mind," she defended instinctively. But a whisper of doubt trailed behind that statement—*he wouldn't, would he?*

Her dad's words carried the weight of lifetimes. "Honey, Scott's a patient man, but no husband relishes a wandering wife while he sweats to put bread on the table. Listen to an old-timer's advice—don't take advantage of his kindness, and you'll live a long happy life."

Later, as darkness falls and the neighborhood settles into slumber, Eve lies awake in bed. She dissects that conversation like a cryptic puzzle. Her father's counsel bears the ring of truth, yet it fuels a persistent itch within her—a question whether harmony between freedom and devotion is possible.

Her father had been firm, but consistent, reminding Eve that she can't touch her trust fund until she's thirty-five, as though she'd forgotten. Her parents have cut off all support on account of her marrying Scott, and the transition from an heiress to a middle-class housewife has not been without its difficulties. Eve's family is not happy with her for marrying "beneath her means," and Eve is aware she must endure her punishment, at least in the short term.

It isn't even that she wants to visit Lucy in Hawaii, as much as it is that she wants to prove her sister wrong, to prove she is still adventurous, that she still could. Instead, her father's words claw at her insides like a caged beast: *wandering desires do not an ideal housewife make.*

This might have been true for her mother, but it won't be true for Eve. She tells herself that everything is available, always. And Scott is *not* her father.

But as the night wears on, doubt slips in, tiptoeing through the gaps in her conviction.

In the shadows of their bedroom, Eve makes a decision. She will book a flight and tell Scott about it in the morning.

2

The rain descends in a gentle drizzle, transforming the sleepy town into a canvas of pensive beauty. Seeking refuge, Eve ducks into a local shop, the doorbell's soft chime urging her out of the grayness.

"Can I help you find something?" the clerk, an older woman with kind eyes, inquires from behind the counter.

"Just browsing, thank you," Eve says, her eyes scanning the cozy shop.

As she wanders through the aisles, her gaze flits to the 'Help Wanted' board at the back of the store. Wouldn't that just show her father? His oldest daughter, the first in their family to work a menial job in generations. Eve can't help herself; she keeps coming back to this board, but then again, she has never found earning an honest day's pay beneath her. Though, truth be told, she also cannot know the lengths to which people must often betray themselves in order to keep that steady paycheck.

Amid the various listings of lost cats and yard work flyers, her eyes catch sight of an intriguing ad: "Longing for more?" It is pinned among mundane business cards, and a strange sense of curiosity nudges her. She hesitates for a moment, pondering its meaning, then takes out her phone and scans the QR code on the flyer. A teenager stocking shelves catches Eve's eye. She smiles and shoves her phone in her purse and continues on her way.

Later, she exchanges pleasantries with the clerk while paying for her paperback, scented candle, and pack of gum, their fleeting words lingering in the air. Beneath Eve's composed smile, hints of uneasiness stir within her. The charming routine of Oak Hollow's days can feel confining at times. Eve loves it here, mostly because Scott loves it here, and she knows it's not forever. Eventually, Scott will warm up to the job offer her father has presented and the two of them will move back to the city. Or maybe not. Maybe Scott is right. Maybe Eve will get so used to small-town living that she can't possibly imagine herself anywhere else. She doubts it with her whole heart, but as her father likes to say: stranger things have happened. After all, in his eyes, she married a broke cowboy. Those were his exact words when she told him the news.

This is not the way Eve sees it, of course. But then, money doesn't matter so much when it's something you've always had. This is probably one of the few things her dad and Scott actually agree on.

Leaving the shop, the rain has subsided, the streets quiet. As she walks back to her car, she can't shake off the unspoken question of the cryptic ad.

In the comfort of her car, she pulls out her phone, checking her email for the hundredth time. There resides the defiant secret —the plane ticket for her upcoming trip, a chance to prove to Lucy, and mostly to herself, that she is still spontaneous.

Pocketing her phone, Eve drives home, soaking up the sleepy beauty around her, separate from the ordinary rhythms of her new life here. She considers stopping at the general store to ask about the 'Help Wanted' sign in the window but decides against another rejection. Oak Hollow has a penchant for nepotism, and the last three rejections tell Eve that she has not yet earned her place.

This is the first time in her thirty-two years that Eve has not been able to wave her hand and have her latest whim, but even so, it's less about the money as it is that she needs something to fill the time. Scott puts in long hours working as a legal assistant at his uncle's law firm, and Eve has always been someone for whom it does not suit to have idle hands. She longs to meet people—to fit in here—to prove her family wrong. But so far, no dice.

For starters, the townsfolk have not taken kindly to her and Scott's renovations. The neighbors see it as a personal offense, referring to it as the beginning of gentrification. The community has not been quiet about their distaste, the whispers of who Eve's father is and the speculation around her sizable trust fund have been quite loud.

As her house appears through the fog, Eve's thoughts grow heavy. The decades-old split level holds potential, but many renovations await—peeling wallpaper, creaky floors, leaky pipes. Each stubborn task is a reminder of time and patience in short supply. She wonders if the neighbors are right...maybe the status quo isn't so bad. Maybe she shouldn't have listened to Scott; maybe buying a fixer upper wasn't the best idea. But the truth is, they had different ideas about what a fixer upper was. Eve couldn't have fathomed living in a place like this before she met Scott. Now, she doesn't want to hurt his feelings. And besides, it would be wholly unnecessary. Eve has learned from experience: throw enough money at a problem and nearly everything becomes fixable.

Unlocking the door, she enters the stillness within, tidying and reorganizing to pass the time, whatever it takes not to call the plumber for the third time today. He does not appreciate Eve's calls any more than she appreciates having to make them. Eve has yet to realize that not everyone in Oak Hollow is as motivated by the dollar as they are where she's from—nor is the choice of plumbers as readily available.

Shadows grow as afternoon fades to dusk. She glances at the

clock, counting down until Scott returns from his long day at the firm.

The rain continues falling in a gentle drizzle as Eve starts dinner. The mundane chores do little to distract her restless mind. She'd meant to tell Scott about her trip this morning, had laid in bed staring at the ceiling, waiting for him to wake. But then he did, running his hand up her thigh, and within seconds, Eve's mind had turned to putty. *Later,* she thought.

She glances out the window, watching the raindrops slide down the glass. Each droplet follows the same path, merging into little rivers that flow steadily downward. Eve envies their singular focus. Her own thoughts move in a hundred different directions, tugging her toward an endless to-do list. The secret trip still waits for Scott's return from the office, poised on the tip of her tongue.

Part of her yearns to confess to Scott, to speak her defiance into reality. But the practical part wants to hold back, wary of disappointing him and further disrupting progress on their renovations.

When she finally hears the garage door opening, Eve freezes. Scott enters, shaking the rain from his coat. His weariness is evident in the sag of his shoulders, the furrow between his brows.

"Rough day?" Eve asks, taking his jacket.

Scott sighs, running a hand through his damp hair. "The usual. How about you?"

"Oh, nothing exciting," Eve lies. "Just chores and errands."

Scott nods, already drifting toward the living room and the comfort of the couch. Eve follows him, the trip still dancing on her tongue, begging to be spoken into existence. "I'm exhausted," he says, kissing her mouth. "Dinner ready?"

"Almost."

Later, as they eat, Eve studies Scott's face in the soft light. She knows he hates his job; she is aware that his uncle is not the easiest person to work for. Scott frequently mentions that being a "paper pusher" is not his ultimate aim in life and Eve knows he longs to start his own business, but after his last endeavor went under, he has neither the capital nor the heart.

Looking at him now, she aches to just spit it out, to give shape to the thoughts that left her sleepless last night. But each time she tries, the words snag in her throat. He's already dealing with so much. So she swallows them down again, keeping her secret close. She will carry its weight a little longer…just until the right moment reveals itself.

For now, it is enough just to have him home, the two of them listening to the gentle rain outside. Eve knows he's beat because he hasn't asked about the plumber yet. They've tiptoed around the topic of construction, sticking to safer, more amenable topics.

Then later, when Scott, tired but grinning, asks her to join him for a shower, she doesn't hesitate for a second, the haunting words from the flyer suddenly echoing through her mind: *Longing for more?*

Eve smiles as she steps into the steamy shower, Scott's powerful arms encircling her waist. As water cascades over them, Eve leans into his sturdy frame, all other concerns dissolving away. Scott kisses her neck and murmurs, "I love you" into her ear.

Eve sighs contentedly. *Longing for more?* She has everything she could ever want right here. As Scott's hands travel lower, Eve closes her eyes, losing herself in his familiar touch.

Telling him about the trip can wait one more day, she decides. Tomorrow morning over coffee, she will tell him about her impulsive decision, explain her growing restlessness, express her disappointment that everyone in this town seems to have made up their minds about her, and admit the plumber has stopped taking her calls. But for now, with Scott's body pressed against hers, Eve lets the warm water wash her doubts away.

It's fine, she thinks as Scott's lips find hers. I can tell him tomorrow.

3

Eve's eyes snap open. For a disoriented moment, she reaches across the rumpled sheets, expecting to find Scott's warm body next to hers. But his side of the bed is empty, the imprint of his head still visible on the pillow.

When she sits up, her stomach drops. The clock reveals it's already nine—Scott has left for work without waking her, a reminder of their early days together. Regret surges through Eve; they haven't had a chance to talk. She'd wanted to tell him about the contractor and the trip, to explain the desperate need to go.

Dragging herself out of the comforting cocoon of blankets, Eve feels the frigid hardwood floor under her bare feet. A hot coffee is the only remedy for the bone-deep chill that has settled upon her.

As the coffee brews, the rich aroma fills the quiet kitchen, the silence interrupted only by the distant hum of a lawnmower outside.

Grabbing her phone from the half-finished countertop, Eve finds a new text from Scott: *Hey babe, sorry I had to rush out early this morning. I know things have been hectic, but I want you to know I love you with all my heart. Could you pick up a few things for dinner if you're out today? Was thinking I could make that spinach and mushroom pasta primavera you love so much tonight. Maybe we could open that nice bottle of Cabernet we've been saving. xo*

Hugging the phone to her chest, warmth floods through Eve. Touched by Scott's thoughtfulness, she types back: *That sounds perfect. Can't wait. Love you so much. x*

The coffee finishes brewing with a final gurgle. Eve fills her favorite oversized mug, wrapping her hands around it to warm her chilled fingers. The first sip is scalding, but rich and smooth—exactly what she needs. She takes a deep breath, feeling lighter as the caffeine hits her bloodstream.

After a long shower, Eve returns to the closet wrapped in a fluffy white towel. Goosebumps prickle her damp skin in the cool air as she chooses jeans and a chunky sweater, in case it turns chilly later. She pulls her long brown hair up into a messy ponytail, wispy tendrils framing her face. A swipe of mascara and lip gloss, and she is ready to tackle the day. She has dozens of construction calls and emails to return and hundreds of design decisions to make. She also needs to attend to Scott's request and good thing, because Eve just realized they're nearly out of coffee creamer.

Later that afternoon, upon arriving at the grocery store, an eerie quiet greets Eve. Only a few shoppers slowly wander the aisles, the fluorescent lights lending a sterile feel. Eve grabs a small cart and starts checking items off Scott's list: ripe tomatoes, fresh basil, garlic, a wedge of parmesan.

As she turns down the pasta aisle, a disheveled older man catches her eye. Dressed in a dingy mechanic's uniform, greasy, gray hair limp over his forehead, he stares intently at the sauces. The name patch embroidered on his shirt catches her eye; it has been scratched off. He turns, frowning at Eve. He mumbles something, shakes his head, and then looks away, shuffling down the aisle with hunched shoulders.

A prickle of unease creeps up the back of her neck, but she brushes it off as a twitchy reaction to stress. Hurrying through the list, Eve constantly glances over her shoulder. She can't shake the feeling of being watched, of the man tracking her every move.

By the time she reaches the checkout and then the parking lot, Eve feels a pit in her stomach. In the late afternoon stillness, she feels increasingly unsettled, shadows stretching long across the vacant lot. She's loading the last bag into the trunk of her Mercedes when a gravelly voice calls out from behind her, "Sorry to bother you, miss."

Whirling around with a gasp, Eve sees the man from inside shuffling out of an old green pickup next to her. Her stomach knots with sudden terror. She brushes it off. Like everyone is always saying, nothing ever happens in Oak Hollow, something Eve agrees with, though her interpretation is more literal than the locals.

When the man reaches her, he keeps his eyes on his scuffed boots. "I'm just a bit hard of hearing after a minor stroke a couple years ago," he mumbles, gesturing to his right arm hanging at his side.

Frozen beside her car, Eve shifts her body for a quick getaway. Her heart picks up speed as she stares warily at the man, unsure what he wants.

"I noticed you in the store earlier," he continues, his voice raspy. "Didn't mean to alarm you with my bumblings. These strokes, they addle the mind something awful." He taps his forehead with a yellowed fingernail. "Makes me forget my manners around pretty young ladies such as yourself."

Eve's skin crawls at being called "pretty" by this man. She takes a subtle step back, desperate to get away but not wanting to provoke him.

Oblivious to her revulsion, he rambles on. "Was hoping a sweet gal like you could help me load some heavy cases of bottled water into my truck. These old bones just don't work like they used to."

Despite every instinct screaming at her to run, Eve feels a twinge of sympathy for his disability. Her eyes dart toward her cart, her purse and phone in it. Her phone rings. She sees Lucy's face pop up on the screen.

The man loses his footing and nearly tumbles to the ground.

"Um. Sure," she finds herself saying, her eyes shifting to his grocery cart, then her phone and back. She turns to grab a case of water bottles, ignoring the call and her racing heart. Too late, she notices the man's gnarled hand slipping into his pocket.

A sharp prick hits Eve's neck. Her legs buckle as the fast-acting sedative takes hold. The man lowers her limp body to the oil-stained pavement.

"Shhh now, just relax," he croons. "Ol' Jenkins is gonna take good care of you." Rough hands grip Eve's ankles, dragging her toward the back of the old green pickup. Her vision blurs at the dingy white camper shell on the bed of the truck.

He heaves her numb body into the dark, musty camper like a bag of garbage, then climbs in after her. Plastic zip ties bite into her wrists and ankles as she is trussed up on the cold metal floor. Eve feels herself floating in and out of consciousness.

Through the closing camper doors, the man leers down at her, his yellowed teeth flashing in a grin. He stuffs a dirty rag in her mouth and slaps tape over it. "We're gonna have some fun, you and me. Just gotta get you back to my special little playroom first."

With that, he slams the doors, sealing Eve in darkness. The truck engine roars to life, carrying her away like a bad dream. Eve thrashes against her bindings, screaming soundlessly against the gag and the sedative coursing through her veins. She strains until her throat is raw, until she is choking, praying someone will hear her silent cries.

"I see we've got ourselves a fighter." The man lets out a wicked laugh. "My favorite kind."

Eve might be too trusting, but she is not stupid. She closes her eyes, conserving the strength she knows she'll need. She knows she is well and truly alone—at the mercy of the monster who now holds her captive.

4

Eve's eyes flicker open, immediately assaulted by the light filtering through faded curtains that hang in the pickup's DIY camper shell. She squints against the piercing brightness, each heartbeat pulsating through her skull.

Bound on the cold metal truck bed, she feels every jagged rock the truck hits as it careens recklessly down what must be a dirt road, her body slamming against unforgiving steel. The stale air reeks of motor oil and sickly-sweet pine air freshener, gagging her with its cloying odor but failing to mask the underlying stench of mold and decay.

Eve urgently tugs against the biting zip ties trapping her wrists and ankles. The rough plastic has rubbed her skin raw. Fresh blood trickles down her fingers, slick and hot. Eve can just make out crimson streaks marking the bed of the truck, a thin mattress mere inches from her face, also stained with rust-colored tales of past horrors.

The truck hits a deep rut, slamming Eve's body against the hard metal floor of the crude DIY camper shell installed in the truck bed. She tastes the slick, coppery blood filling her mouth, her lips cut from biting them in a frenzied but useless struggle to break free. Gasping through the pain, Eve's breath hitches as she notices the open sliding rear window between the truck cab and camper.

Ominous tools line the shelves bolted to the camper walls—knives, saws, clamps, pliers—each arranged like surgical instruments. Eve's pulse quickens, imagining them slicing into vulnerable flesh, peeling it back layer by agonizing layer.

"Don't worry, I'll put those to good use soon enough," the man chuckles, a twisted gleam in his eye visible in the rearview mirror.

The truck swerves again, tires skidding wildly on the loose gravel, giving Eve a clear view through the open window of a rusted butcher's cleaver hanging in easy reach.

"You know what they do to people in certain parts of the world—people who touch things that don't belong to them—don't ya?"

Eve closes her eyes and pretends she hasn't heard. She pictures the cleaver hacking through fragile wrist bones and thrashes around, trying to break free. But the unforgiving plastic only bites deeper into her already torn flesh with each frenzied movement.

She has no idea how long they've been driving. *Minutes? Hours?* Panic rising, Eve tries to scream, but the gag stuffed in her mouth muffles any sound. She emits a choked whimper through the tape sealed over her lips.

"Save your breath, doll face. No one's coming to rescue you out here," the man sneers. His voice is like razor blades scraping down her spine.

Sometime later, the truck screeches to a violent halt, its worn tires skidding again before steadying. The doors creak open, and moonlight floods the truck's interior. Eve squints against the darkness, her heart dropping into her stomach.

The man's burly silhouette blots out the meager light as he looms above her. Shadow obscures his features, but the moon glints off his grin, twisted and malevolent. Gnarly hands reach down, the rough texture reminding her of tree bark against her skin. Eve jerks away in vain, the ties biting into her wrists and ankles. She strains against the gag, eliciting only muffled mewls, muted by the tape sealed across her lips.

"Get up, sunshine. We're home," he announces in a singsong voice that turns Eve's blood to ice.

His powerful grip closes around Eve's helpless limbs like iron shackles, dragging her from the truck. Her body flops limply against his thick frame. Eve is dead weight, her limbs still weak from the sedative he'd injected into her neck.

As the man hauls her toward a decrepit cabin nestled among dense forest, the sound of snapping twigs and rustling leaves fills the silence of the forest. Eve hears things scurrying away in the darkness, envying their escape into hidden nooks and crannies.

The man opens the warped wooden door with his shoulder, the swollen frame scraping against it with an agonized creak. As he steps across the threshold, Eve chokes on the stagnant stench of decay and neglect emanating from every surface.

He shoves her inside, and Eve stumbles into the shadowy, unfamiliar space. Grasping for balance, she careens wildly across the dark room. Her shoulder rams hard against the aged hearth of a stone fireplace, skin scraping roughly on soot-stained rock. Gnarly ivy vines snake upward, tendrils reaching to claw at her like skeletal fingers. Their faint, grabbing touch makes Eve shudder, a crawling sensation gliding over her skin.

The inside of the cabin is pitch black, any light from outside unable to penetrate the boarded windows. Eve can just make out the stained, bare mattress on the floor, its surface scattered with mouse droppings and other unnamable filth.

Without warning, the man wrestles Eve's limp body onto the soiled mattress. Her limbs are weak and uncoordinated, offering little resistance against his brute strength. She feels the zip ties loosen, then fall away as he cuts them off her wrists and ankles with a razor-sharp hunting knife. The blade glints as it catches the pale moonlight.

Before Eve can even think to react or struggle, he wrenches her hands behind her back again. The hard metal of handcuffs locks into place, biting into the raw flesh of Eve's wrists. The click of the cuffs locking echoes through the still darkness.

The man presses down on Eve, his weight forcing the breath from her lungs as he brings his cracked lips right to her ear. "There now, all cozy," he rasps, his words filling Eve with convulsive revulsion. "I'm Jenkins, by the way," he says, clamping a dirty hand over her nose and mouth. "Don't worry...you don't need to speak—the pleasure's all mine."

When he finally moves off her, Eve greedily sucks in air. The scream building in her chest dissolves into ragged coughs as she fights not to retch. His shuffling footsteps move away, and the front door creaks open then slams shut. Eve is alone in the icy darkness, at least for now.

She focuses all her energy on struggling to sit up, her surroundings spinning and threatening to plunge her into darkness with even that slight movement. She braces herself against the grimy walls, willing her trembling legs to support her weight. They shake beneath her as she pushes herself to stand, but somehow hold.

Through the lingering sedative haze clouding her mind, Eve struggles to focus...until a scuttling sound from the darkest corner turns her blood to ice. Something is in the cabin with her, concealed by the shadows.

Eve stands paralyzed, listening. There it is again—a sinister skittering and dragging noise, faint but unmistakable.

She strains to see through the darkness, certain something is moving toward her, something primal and ravenous...

5

Eve stands paralyzed as the rustling and dragging noises continue, nearly drowned out by her own hammering heartbeat.

A guttural hiss splits the silence—too primal to be human. The hairs on Eve's neck stand on end as a gray shape detaches itself from the shadows.

Gleaming red eyes reflect the pale moonlight as the creature prowls forward. Eve makes out matted fur and a naked, wormlike tail dragging behind it. Another hiss escapes its pointed snout, exposing curved yellow fangs.

The possum's features materialize from the dark as it approaches Eve. She stumbles back against the grimy wall, her trembling legs barely supporting her weight. It lets out another threatening hiss, strings of saliva dripping from its jaws. The possum fixes its beady eyes on Eve, pure predatory hunger burning behind its piercing gaze.

She recoils as far as the wall allows, her wrists screaming against the cruel bite of the handcuffs. The possum pauses, haunches tensed, as it prepares to lunge at her exposed flesh.

Just then, the cabin door bursts open. The possum's hairless tail thrashes in alarm as it turns to face this new threat. Eve catches a glimpse of Jenkins's imposing form silhouetted in the doorway, the moonlight glinting off the shotgun barrel in his hands.

"Down, Brutus," Jenkins growls. The possum—Brutus— flattens its body against the floor, belly exposed in submission. Its lips peel back in a silent snarl, but it makes no move to attack.

Jenkins steps inside, pumping the shotgun. "You know better than to play with my toys without permission." He aims a kick at the possum's midsection, connecting with a heavy thud. Brutus hisses in pain but keeps his eyes downcast submissively.

Jenkins hooks his thumb over his shoulder. "Get."

Brutus gives Eve one last snarl and glance before scurrying past Jenkins and disappearing into the night.

Jenkins watches him go, then turns to Eve, eyes shining with sick excitement. "Now that the warm-up's done, let's have some real fun."

6

The news footage flickers across the screen, a grainy blur that makes Scott's stomach churn. There's Eve, a small figure crossing and exiting the automatic doors, then crossing the grocery store parking lot, face obscured by shadows and static. Then there's a jump, the footage skips, and she's gone.

Scott grips the arm of the chair, knuckles white. No clear suspect, the reporters say. No one else visible in the frame. His heart hammers against his ribs.

He jumps up, grabs his keys off the counter, and runs for the door, nearly tripping over a pair of Eve's heels left haphazardly on the mat. As he turns the ignition, the engine sputtering to life, his fingers tremble. He needs to talk to Morris, that prick. He needs to make him understand. Eve wouldn't just disappear, not like this.

Tires squeal as he peels out of the driveway, swerving onto the main road. The streets are empty, the town hunkered down as if holding a collective breath. Waiting. Scott presses the gas pedal to the floor, engine roaring. The police station comes into view, a plain squat brick building.

He slams on the brakes outside the station, throwing open the door, slamming it behind him. The soles of his Oxfords slap against the pavement as he dashes inside. An attendant looks up in alarm as Scott slams into the front desk, chest heaving.

"I need to speak to Morris," he says.

The attendant's eyes widen. She picks up the phone, punching in an extension with one red-lacquered nail.

"Detective Morris? Mr. Collins is here about his wife..."

After an excruciating fifty-seven minutes, a gruff voice interrupts Scott's spiraling thoughts. He turns to see the tall detective, face set in hard lines. Morris lifts his chin in greeting to Scott, then beckons him to a nearby door. "Let's talk in here."

Scott follows Blake Morris into a small room. The detective waves him brusquely to a chair, then sits across from him, eyeing him in a way that makes it clear the grudge he holds against Scott is still alive and well, even after all these years.

"I said I'd call if another interview was warranted, so what brings you in?"

Scott leans forward, steepling his fingers under his chin. "You're not taking my wife's disappearance seriously."

"You shouldn't be too worried. As I'm sure you've heard, her father hired his own investigators..."

Scott had not, in fact, heard. "If it were your daughter, wouldn't you do the same?"

"I live on a police salary. He has more money than God... So what do you think, Collins?"

"What do I think?" Scott slams his pointer finger into his chest. "I think what in the hell does your paycheck have to do with Eve? You're either doing your job or you're not—"

"Who are you to tell me how to do my job?"

Scott pinches the bridge of his nose. He's known Blake his whole life, and he knows he'll win more flies with honey. "I'm not telling you—I'm asking you."

Morris scoffs. "Well, in that case—um, yeah—well... since

you're here...why don't you run everything past me one more time."

"You want me to explain everything again?"

Morris nods. "You know, to make sure we're not missing anything...just so it's clear I'm doing my job."

Scott swallows hard. "I already told you—"

"Again," Morris cuts in, flipping open a notebook.

Scott exhales shakily. "Eve left to go grocery shopping two days ago."

"What time?"

"Late afternoon—"

"And when was the last time you heard from her?"

"That morning."

"And she seemed—how?"

"Fine." Scott sighs heavily. This conversation is not going to lead anywhere, and it sure as hell isn't going to bring Eve home. "I told you. We made plans for dinner."

"And then what?"

"And then she didn't come home. I called you myself when she hadn't returned. I knew something was wrong. It's not like Eve not to communicate with me..."

Morris scribbles notes. "And you didn't hear from her at all after she left?"

"No. I tried calling her cell, but it went to voicemail."

"Hm." Morris leans back, regarding Scott coolly. "Well, I guess I ought to tell you...we've uncovered some new information that's...well, it's, um...concerning."

Scott stiffens. "What do you mean? What information?"

"Your wife recently booked a plane ticket to Hawaii. Did you know about that?"

Scott looks away and then back at Morris. "Her sister lives there."

"But you weren't aware of it?"

"She mentioned Lucy wanting her to fly out—but Eve said she had too much on her plate..."

Morris's eyes bore into him. "So your wife secretly booked a solo vacation and now she's disappeared. That doesn't strike you as odd?"

"It wasn't really a secret. Like I said, her sister lives there."

"And yet, she hadn't told you..."

Scott's voice shakes. "She hadn't given me a tentative date, no."

"Maybe this is her way of getting away from you for a while," Morris suggests. "Maybe there were problems in your marriage you weren't aware of."

"Are you saying she's in Hawaii?"

"I'm not saying anything."

Scott's hands curl into fists under the table. "My wife was abducted," he says, his teeth clenched. "She wouldn't just wander off without the car, her purse, or her phone. Something happened to her."

Morris holds up a hand placatingly. "I understand your concern, Collins. But we have to consider all possibilities in a missing persons case. Ruling things out systematically is part of the process." He stands and brushes the legs of his trousers. "And you know how women can be, especially rich ones."

"No, Morris. I don't know how women can be. Why don't you enlighten me?"

"I sure hope this is the first lie you've told in this interview, Collins. Because everybody in this town knows you've always been quite the ladies' man."

Scott rests his head in his hands. Some grudges can last a lifetime, and this seems to be one of them.

"I assume you've said what you came to say," Morris says after a long beat. He doesn't wait for a response. "In that case—we'll be in touch if we need anything else."

Scott stalks out, nearly shaking with rage. Morris and the other so-called cops in this town are wasting time when Eve is out there, missing. The writing is on the wall. They clearly aren't going to be of much use.

Thank God his father-in-law had hired *real* detectives. But that left one question, why hadn't he mentioned this to Scott? And why hadn't Eve told him about her trip to Hawaii?

7

Time slips by in a tortuous trickle as Eve fades in and out of an uneasy unconsciousness. She catches only fragments of her surroundings—the ominous creaking of floorboards, the spine-tingling scratching of unseen creatures in shadowy corners, the raspy off-key humming drifting occasionally through the still air.

An aggressive growl in Eve's empty stomach wrests her violently from the drug's grip. Her eyelids drag themselves open, vision blurry and strained against the weak light filtering through gaps in the cabin's boarded windows. She blinks slowly, willing her surroundings to come into focus.

Eve startles fully awake at the sound of heavy boots clomping up the porch steps. Her heart begins pounding, adrenaline flooding her system. *Hadn't he just been in the room with her? Hadn't it just been night?* Squinting through the haze, Eve tries to take in details of the room.

The wooden floorboards surrounding her are littered with rotting leaves, animal droppings, and cigarette butts. Faded curtains hang askew over boarded-up windows, blocking any view of the outside world.

A suffocating sense of dread creeps over her as Eve notices sets of thick chains and iron shackles bolted at ominous intervals along the rough timber walls. Their heavy links glint even in the low light, polished by repeated use.

But most chilling are the dozens of yellowed missing persons flyers peeling off the walls around her, overlapping like macabre wallpaper. Photos of fresh-faced young women smile back at Eve with haunting optimism, their descriptions overlapping eerily. Many of their features bear a striking resemblance to her own.

The missing dates scrawled beneath the photos range from months to decades ago. Eve's stomach twists as she realizes she's looking at Jenkins's depraved trophy collection. How long until her face joins these women? Surely, Scott would have called the police by now. Surely, someone at the Harvest Haven would have seen something. It was a rare thing for Eve not to feel she had eyes on her as she moved about Oak Hollow. Why would this time have been any different?

Heavy footsteps sound right outside the door. Eve flinches as it swings open with an agonized groan. Jenkins's form fills the entryway, blocking the weak sunlight. The overpowering smell of stale beer, body odor, and halitosis hits Eve. She recoils instinctively.

"Rise and shine, princess." Jenkins's gravelly baritone cuts through the thick air. He ambles closer, each footfall seeming to echo through Eve's skull. He looms over her, his tall frame enshrouding her in shadow. Eve twists against the handcuffs binding her wrists, the unforgiving metal biting into her raw flesh. They refuse to give even a centimeter.

Jenkins trails a filthy, overgrown fingernail lazily down Eve's cheek, leaving a wet streak on her skin. "Ain't you the prettiest new addition," he remarks, as if admiring a new pet.

Revulsion claws up Eve's throat as his fetid breath washes over her. She longs to snap her teeth into Jenkins's gnarled hand, to tear flesh from bone, but her parched mouth can only manage a choking whimper.

Reading her impotent rage, Jenkins chuckles. "Got some fight left in ya, I see. I like that." With a sadistic grin, he grabs the handcuffs and rattles them against each other right next to Eve's ears. The grating metal reverberates through her skull.

"Don't worry, you'll settle down soon enough. They all do."

Eve's gaze darts to the dozens of shining faces smiling from the walls - all those other girls who came here with fight left in them too. She wonders how long each one clung to that fire before Jenkins extinguished it forever. Eve knows, even in the fog of being drugged, the statistics for missing persons. The odds are not looking good, and she realizes the gravity of her situation.

“Thought I’d keep you company,” he says.

Eve watches as Jenkins shuffles toward an ancient TV set in the corner. He twists a knob, and it flickers to life. Its grainy glow lights his face with a ghostly pallor, casting twisting shadows that seamlessly blend with the cabin's natural gloom. The static laugh track of some decades-old sitcom fills the silence, mingling with Jenkins's perpetual humming. He plops down on a grimy loveseat and fixes on the screen, his rheumy eyes glazed and thoughts clearly somewhere far away.

Seizing the opportunity of his distraction, Eve scans the cabin, searching for anything she could use as a weapon or means of escape. There are the chains, but then, she’s handcuffed.

In one corner sits an ancient pot-bellied stove, its door hanging open to reveal only a cold empty space within. Fishing nets hang from the rafters, collecting cobwebs.

The whole cabin reeks of decay and neglect—rotting wood, mildew, and rodent leavings. The peeling flyers reveal gnawed exposed laths underneath. Eve imagines the whole derelict structure must be infested with all manner of pests that thrive in darkness and ruin. She thinks of Brutus and shudders. She can’t believe people actually live like this.

Jenkins stirs, heaving himself up from the sagging couch with a chorus of creaking joints. Eve's muscles involuntarily tense. She thinks again of the knives and tools lining the shelves in Jenkins's camper, just outside. If only she could get free and arm herself...

But the handcuffs refuse to yield, only biting deeper into her skin. He shuffles toward her, each footfall seeming to echo with ominous finality through the dead quiet. Jenkins runs a rough, grimy thumb over Eve's split and swollen bottom lip.

"Those sweet lips say you're thirsty. Let ol' Jenkins get you a nice drink." His voice drips with mock sincerity. Before Eve can jerk away, he grasps her jaw with bruising force, fingernails digging into her cheek as he forces her face upward. His cold eyes lock with hers, a twisted grin forming on his lips. "Say please," he sneers, reveling in the power he exerts over her. "What's happened to your manners?"

As tears spill from Eve's eyes, she chokes out a muted "please." Jenkins releases her, a cruel satisfaction in his gaze, as if savoring the taste of submission.

Eve watches as he goes to pump murky water from the old iron sink into a chipped glass. She eyes it warily as he returns, half expecting some fresh horror or drugging. But ultimately, her parched mouth wins out over her suspicion.

Jenkins presses the cold glass to her lips, and Eve guzzles the water down, not caring when some spills over her torn sweater. Even dirty and bitter, it soothes her raw throat.

As the last drops slide down, Eve gasps for air. Jenkins remains crouched before her, balancing on the balls of his feet as he watches her intently. His bloodshot eyes travel over Eve's body, like a wolf admiring its cornered prey. Jenkins slowly runs his tongue over his thin, cracked lips.

When he speaks, his voice comes out low and throbbing with twisted excitement. "You know, me and my Edna used to have some real fun together. You remind me of her... spittin' image, I tell ya." He smiles so wide his gums show. "Ain't it the damnedest thing?"

8

The implication hits Eve's gut like a brick. Her stomach twists violently, and she jerks away from Jenkins. But his scarred hand darts out quicker, knotting in her hair and wrenching Eve's face back toward his.

"Uh-uh-uh," Jenkins chides, clicking his tongue. Eve strikes out in sudden fury, raking her nails across the back of his hand, landing a kick to his groin. Jenkins retaliates with a lightning-fast backhand that snaps Eve's head to the side. White spots explode across her vision. She blinks through swimming tears to see a crimson stain blossoming on her shirt sleeve where the handcuff has cut into her wrist.

When her eyes refocus, Jenkins's face looms mere inches away. His expression is dark with barbaric rage, spittle collecting at the corner of his contorted mouth. "That's the last time you'll show me disrespect, princess," he snarls, a guttural note in his voice that terrifies Eve to her core.

"Keep that pretty skin of yours intact, if you know what's good for you." Jenkins brings his face even closer, forcing Eve to choke on his rancid breath. "You're going to learn your place right quick. And your new place is under me."

The suggestive threat in his gravelly voice makes Eve's stomach turn. As Jenkins draws back, his lips peel into a yellowed grin that fails to reach his cold, empty eyes. A fresh wave of panic crashes over Eve, a stark reminder of her complete and utter helplessness at his hands.

Jenkins turns his back, and Eve releases a ragged breath. Her mind races as she wrestles against the cuffs, trying to pacify her panic. She thinks of Scott, imagines him searching for her, and promises herself she will find a way back to him or die trying. Her father will find her. By now, he will have called upon the best of the best. He has immense resources at his beck and call, and even though he and Eve have not exactly seen eye to eye lately, Eve knows he will never give up. He will go to the ends of the earth, if that's what it takes. Scott, too. Eve has to believe this. It's all she has.

"I can pay you," she says. "My family, we can pay—whatever you need."

"Pay?" Jenkins mouth gapes open. He looks absolutely dumbfounded; his striking eyes wide with disbelief. "Pay me for what?"

"For letting me go. Ransom—"

Jenkins lets out a guttural laugh, throwing his head back as his whole body shakes with inexplicable amusement. "What do I need money for?" he says, sweeping one arm out to gesture around the dilapidated cabin, a cruel grin twisting his cracked lips. "I've already got everything I want right here, princess."

"But what if it was a lot?" Eve manages. "Whatever you want, I'm sure—"

Jenkins regards her carefully, his eyes narrowing in consideration as he strokes his unshaven chin. He takes a few slow, deliberate steps toward Eve, his imposing frame looming over her. Leaning down, he places one large, calloused hand on either side of where she sits, trapping her. Eve feels sick as he stares intensely into her eyes. When he speaks, his voice comes out low and threatening. "You have a lot to learn, sweet thing."

Jenkins straightens up to his full height, his shadow engulfing Eve. He cracks his knuckles menacingly. "Money can't buy everything."

His eyes blaze with sudden fury, and he leans in close again, grabbing Eve's chin in his rough hand, forcing her to meet his terrifying gaze. "And if you know what's good for you..." He squeezes harder, his fingernails digging crescents into her skin. "You won't mention it again."

The shadows around her seem to twitch and flex as Jenkins putters around the cabin. She can't tear her eyes away from him, tracking his every movement like a prisoner watching the swinging ax that will end her.

The wait is interminable torture. Eve knows with bone-deep certainty that when Jenkins turns his full attention back to her, it will mean only pain and debasement.

His shuffling footsteps stop. The creak of a closet door opening. The clinking of metal and glass. Eve's heart seizes—her gut tells her this is where her nightmare transcends to hell.

Jenkins turns, his gnarled hands clutching various sinister instruments—a long gleaming knife, coils of rough rope, a bottle of clear liquid. His eyes fix on Eve, burning with depraved intent.

"Time to see what you're made of, sweetheart," he rasps.

Eve thrashes against the handcuffs, the unforgiving metal slicing her wrists yet again. Warm blood trickles down her hand. Jenkins's face splits into a yellowed grin. He advances, each footfall seeming to drive nails into Eve's coffin. Then he stops and appears to stumble.

His eyes widen as he violently shakes his head. He begins slapping his palm against his forehead over and over, until finally he stops and his eyes land on Eve. "Oh, Edna. My darling Edna. Look at you. What have I done?"

9

The instruments fall from Jenkins's limp grasp, clattering to the cabin floor as his face contorts in anguish. "Edna, my love, oh, God, dear Lord, not again," he whimpers, shaking hands clutching at his tangled hair. "I've done it again, haven't I?"

Eve watches, heart hammering with mingled hope and fear as Jenkins crumbles before her. She tenses, poised for anything in the unpredictable pendulum swing of his moods.

Jenkins's eyes brim with tears as he gazes at Eve with dawning horror. "Look at you. You're hurt..." he croaks, his ragged voice cracking. He reaches a trembling hand toward her handcuffed wrist, faltering just shy of bloodied skin. "Let me help you."

Eve cranes away, pulse racing at having the devil this close, but the cuffs hold her fast. She flinches as his too-gentle fingers examine her raw wounds, unable to reconcile this sudden compassion from the man she witnessed just seconds ago.

"You shouldn't suffer this way, my love." Tears prick the corners of his eyes. "Edna, you know I didn't mean any of this."

Jenkins's wavering words feel like whip cracks in Eve's ears. She watches him through tangled strands of hair, searching for an angle in this abrupt transformation, already planning to use his delusion to manipulate an escape.

"Let's get you cleaned up, my darling," Jenkins says, producing a key and freeing her throbbing wrists from bondage.

Eve rises unsteadily, shaking limbs barely supporting her weight, as Jenkins guides her toward the cabin door. The forest beckons, impossibly out of reach. Eve casts a last frightened glance back at the missing girls adorning the squalid walls—so many who never found freedom. She promises herself she will not share their fate.

Scott is searching for her. Her family is searching. Eve thinks of her mother—of Lucy—and she feels sick. Her stomach turns, but her resolve straightens.

The cabin door creaks open, and Eve steps into the cool air, keenly aware of the predator at her back.

She has plans to run the first chance she gets.

She doesn't even make it to the shed. After half a dozen steps, Eve blacks out.

She wakes to damp concrete chilling her skin as Jenkins places her limp body onto the cold floor. Confusion clouds her mind through the haze of sedatives. This shed, isolated deep in the woods, is an unlikely place for Jenkins to bring her. Eve shivers, acutely aware of her vulnerability.

Jenkins grasps the shower handle with his wrinkled hand and a stream of frigid water rains down. Eve flinches and folds into a ball, a futile attempt to shield herself.

"Get up," Jenkins commands.

Eve's limbs feel detached, unresponsive. She wills her body to move through sheer focus, rising slowly to her feet. The water soaks through her tattered clothes, weighing her down.

Jenkins watches her struggle. What sick game is this? One moment a monster, the next almost gentle. Eve searches his pale eyes for clues but finds only madness staring back.

"Take off the clothes," Jenkins orders.

Eve is desperate to run. But Jenkins has proven he can turn violent in an instant. She would have to be clever. And fast. And right now, she is neither. She bends and retches into the drain, falling to her knees. Eve doesn't care what happens next. Let him kill her. Better to get it over with fast. It's obvious she can't outrun him, not like this.

Jenkins peels off her jeans and her sweater, the last items tethering Eve to her old life, then he hands Eve a ragged cloth. "Wash yourself. You smell."

Naked, Eve gets a second wind. She takes the cloth with a shaking hand. The water chills her to the bone, but she scrubs dutifully. Jenkins nods in approval.

"Good girl. I'll return with fresh clothes." Jenkins walks out, and Eve seizes her chance. She lunges for the shed door.

Suddenly, a voice rings out, stopping Eve in her tracks. "Don't do it," the voice says. "It's a trap. He'll shoot you as soon as you run."

Eve freezes.

"This is his twisted idea of a sport," the voice says. "Stalking prey he has let believe is free."

Eve takes a step forward.

"He likes to go for the kneecap, just so you know..."

She stops. Something in the woman's voice tells her this is not a lie.

Jenkins returns with a smile, humming an unfamiliar tune. Eve hides her desperation beneath a mask of compliance as he tosses a pile of clothes at her feet. "Get dressed. Don't keep me waiting."

Jenkins disappears behind the door.

Eve's skin crawls at the thought of wearing the clothing he has given her, a woman's housecoat that looks as though it was last worn about three decades ago. But she has no choice, and she'd rather have something rather than nothing. She dresses in Jenkins's offerings, all too big on her frame.

Eve's eyes dart around the shed, seeking anything to aid her escape. But the room is barren. No tools, no weapons, nothing.

Except the vent. Eve notices it now, tucked away in the corner. It's where the voice came from.

Eve creeps closer. She can hear faint whispers from within. There's another room off the shed, a grated vent has been installed in the wall between it and the shower.

"Hello?" Eve whispers. "Is someone there?"

"Yes," comes the hushed reply. "I'm here."

"You're there?" Eve's heart leaps. She isn't alone. "My name is Eve."

"First couple of days are the worst, keep that in mind…"

"How long have you been here?"

"Too long," she whispers bitterly.

Eve's eyes close. "What's your name?"

"Mira."

Footsteps outside. Their brief connection is severed as Jenkins returns. Eve hides her curiosity as he grabs her and places the cuffs on her wrists.

"Time to go back," he announces with a leer, his mood shifting again. Eve glances back once at the vent, Mira's voice replaying in her mind. *It's a trap.*

She takes a deep breath to steady herself as Jenkins drags her toward the cabin. But then he appears to change his mind and they start toward the house.

"Now that you're clean," he says, "Edna won't mind."

"Edna?"

Jenkins stops and looks at her through hooded lids and lets out an exasperated sigh. "Edna is my wife."

10

Scott stares again at the grainy security footage, his mind racing. Eve's dark hair and petite frame are unmistakable, even in the blurry images. She's loading groceries into her car, glancing around nervously. Then she's gone, vanished from the frame.

"There must be more footage," Scott says to Reed. "Clearly, you can see something is wrong."

Reed shakes his head. Scott is grateful to him for coming over this late; he could tell Reed was hesitant. "This is all we've got. No other cameras captured the parking lot."

Scott grips the back of the armchair in his living room, knuckles white. Helplessness washes over him.

"We're doing everything we can to find her," Reed says. His tone is clipped, professional, not at all like the friend Scott has known since preschool. Scott searches Reed's face for any glimmer of hope or compassion but finds little.

Desperation edges in Scott's voice. "I know my wife, Reed. She wouldn't just disappear like this. Someone has taken her."

Reed nods but his eyes betray doubt. "We're pursuing every lead. But there's no evidence of foul play—at least not yet. This isn't CSI, bud—these things don't get resolved at the snap of your fingers."

Scott glances back at the pixelated image of his wife's face. A grim determination settles over him. He'll scour every inch of this town if that's what it takes.

"Why didn't you know about the plane ticket she purchased?" Reed asks, his tone sharp at first, but when he looks at Scott, he changes his tune. "I mean, Morris says you didn't know."

Scott shakes his head. "We don't usually discuss minor purchases like that."

"A trip to Hawaii, though? That seems like a major thing to hide from your spouse," Reed chimes in skeptically.

Scott's jaw tightens. "Things have been hectic lately. With the renovations and all…" His voice trails off. He feels a twinge of shame admitting this to Reed. "We've had other things to discuss…"

"Yeah, I bet..." Reed says casually, not seeming to put much thought into his words.

"What if one of the workers took her?" Scott asks. "So many guys have been in and out..." He pauses. "Did you interview those people I told Morris about?"

Reed's tone remains casual. "It's only been a few days, Collins..."

"Two days is a fucking eternity. Imagine it was Claire."

Reed scoffs as he flippantly says, "Doubtful. Claire can't even go to the bathroom without notifying me first."

"You think this is funny?" Fury rises in Scott at the thoughtlessness. "Is my wife's disappearance a joke to you?"

Reeds leans forward. "No, of course not."

He sighs, then levels his gaze at Scott. "I'm sure you want to find her. We all do. I mean, look—you called and I came. I'm just trying to get the full picture…but honestly, man? It's an active investigation—I really shouldn't even be here."

Scott rubs his temples, emotions swirling. He wants to trust

Reed, but his tone implies Eve left him—or worse, that Scott's a suspect. And of course, he would be. Scott knows this.

Even so, Scott can see Reed doesn't *actually* suspect foul play. He thinks Eve left him, bound for greener pastures, just like everyone said she would.

Still, Reed and Morris—all of them—they'd have to be blind and stupid to think Eve—or *any* woman— would just leave a cart full of groceries, their purse, phone, and keys, and just vanish.

"You're right," Scott says finally. He understands his limitations, knows he has to remain cordial. He has to cooperate if he intends to find Eve. Bridges are easily burned in this town, something Scott knows all too well.

"Okay, look. Maybe I don't know everything that was going on with her lately," he admits wearily. "But I know Eve. She wouldn't just run off. Something happened to her. And I need you to take this seriously, Reed."

"And I am. Of course, I am." Reed nods, but his eyes remain clouded with doubt. "We all are."

Scott's stomach twists. He sees now that even his childhood best friend won't be his ally. If he wants answers, he'll have to find them himself.

11

Eve's mind races as he drags her toward the house. He has a wife. She doesn't know what to say—anything could set off his explosive temper. "Do you want me to meet her?"

"Later," he says. "Once you've suffered a little more. Edna doesn't like it when I bring pretty girls around. She might make me kill you before I'm ready. You know how women are…"

Eve swallows hard at his words, then decides to test him. "Please, don't hurt me," she says. "I'll do whatever you want."

Jenkins sneers, his grip tightening on her arm. "You'll do whatever I want, regardless. But it's more fun when you struggle."

He shoves her through the back door and into the kitchen. Eve scans the room, looking for potential weapons or escape routes, and of course, for any sign of Edna. But the empty room, the heavy door and barred windows, leave little hope.

Jenkins forces her into a chair and binds her ankles. Eve focuses on keeping her breathing even, hiding her rising panic. She has to stay alert, wait for any opening.

"Are you hungry?" Jenkins asks, his tone mocking. "You must be, after such a long trek. Edna and me, we don't get many visitors up here. 'Specially not this time of year."

He grabs an apple from the counter and takes a large bite. Eve's stomach growls at the sight of food, but she stays silent.

"Here." Jenkins holds the apple to her lips. Eve hesitates, then takes a small bite. She needs to keep up her strength. More importantly, she needs to gain his trust.

Jenkins nods in approval, then pulls the apple back and devours the rest. He leaves Eve bound to the chair, her hunger somehow worse with the single bite, as he moves beyond her line of sight.

Eve's mind races. She has to find a way to overpower Jenkins, to get out of here. She thinks of Mira.

How long have you been here? Too long.

She cannot end up like the girls on the walls of that cabin. Patience has never been a virtue of Eve's, and she doesn't intend to start now.

She strains against the ropes binding her ankles, but they hold fast. The chair creaks as she shifts her weight, trying to find any give in her constraints.

Jenkins is whistling as he moves about the house, the mundane domesticity of it sending a chill through Eve. The normalcy of an apple, restraints on a kitchen chair—what is his plan?

Eve's breath catches as she hears Jenkins's boots scuff closer. Her palms sweat against the handcuffs.

When Jenkins finally steps into view, Eve's heart seizes. With hungry relish, Jenkins fingers the jagged, serrated edge of the blade in his hand. Her mind screams warnings, but her fatigued limbs can barely struggle against their bonds. Jenkins's dead eyes fix on her with chilling delight as he turns the weapon, admiring its glint. "It's time for your branding."

"No—"

"We must. Edna says so…says you're all like cattle…"

He takes slow, deliberate steps closer, and Eve squeezes her eyes shut, bracing for searing pain. She waits, pulse thundering in her ears. But instead of wet heat blooming from tore flesh, she feels nothing. Instead of carving the blade into her, when Eve opens her eyes, Jenkins has begun slicing an apple. He carefully cuts thin pieces, the juice dripping down his hands.

"Open up," he commands, holding a slice to Eve's mouth. "Need to feed you first. Can't have you passing out on me, 'cause you can't sleep here. You know what they say…happy wife, happy life."

She clamps her lips shut and turns her head away. Jenkins's hand shoots out, grabbing her jaw and wrenching it back to face him.

"I said open."

The knife glints as he brings it near her eye. Eve reluctantly parts her lips, and Jenkins pops the apple slice into her mouth.

"There's a good girl," he purrs, stroking her hair. Eve fights the urge to spit the apple in his face.

Jenkins continues feeding her slices, seeming to relish having her at his mercy. Eve's mind turns to Mira, thinking she should have asked her more questions. She should have asked Mira how she's managed to survive, because with the way Jenkins is looking at her, Eve is not sure she wants to.

"What do you say?" he asks as Eve swallows the last slice of apple, the sweetness turning bitter in her mouth.

"Thank you," she whispers, keeping her eyes downcast.

Jenkins looks pleased. "You're learning. A fast learner, too. Edna will be pleased."

"When can I meet her?" Eve asks, though after the words are out, she's not sure she should have.

"Soon enough. She really doesn't like when people overstay their welcome, so we have to be careful."

He unties the ropes binding her wrists and ankles. Eve suppresses a shudder as his rough hands make contact with her skin.

"Let's get you back to the cabin. It's almost time for your medicine."

Medicine. The word makes Eve's stomach knot. She knows it means more drugs to keep her weak and compliant.

"Then we can brand you," he adds, sending Eve's pulse racing. "Easier that way."

As Jenkins leads her out the door and down the rocky path between the main house and the cabin-like structure, Eve's ears strain for any sound from the shed. She hears nothing except the heavy tread of Jenkins's boots behind her.

He opens the cabin door, and Eve steps inside, hugging her arms around herself. Eve senses this small, windowless room is about to become her entire world.

Jenkins prepares a syringe, flicking it with one finger. "This will help you sleep," he says. "Can't have you getting any ideas."

Eve eyes the needle, fear and defiance warring within her. But she has no choice. As the drugs enter her bloodstream, her limbs grow heavy, her thoughts hazy. She clings to one before the darkness claims her and repeats it like a mantra...

Please find me, Scott. I don't want to die.

12

Eve clings to wakefulness as long as she can, but the sedative drags her under despite her efforts. When awareness returns, there is no telling how much time has passed. Her thoughts swim, struggling to orient in a haze of lingering drugs.

Gradually, she becomes aware of a persistent throbbing in her left arm. She blinks against the gloom, eyes focusing on the angry inflamed skin of her bicep. Crude stitches march in ragged rows, spelling out a macabre message: JENKINS'S PROPERTY.

Revulsion twists Eve's gut. While she was unconscious, he carved his ownership of her into her very flesh. Branded her, just as he promised. Marking her like cattle for the slaughter.

Eve grapples against her restraints with renewed panic, but the drugs still paralyze her limbs. She can only watch with building horror as Jenkins enters, clutching a syringe.

"Rise and shine," he grins, flicking the needle. "Can't sleep all day, my pet."

He jabs the syringe into Eve's thigh. She flinches, a whimper escaping her raw throat. Warm numbness spreads, muting the grating rasp of the chains at her wrists.

"There now, just a little something to take the edge off while you heal," Jenkins croons. "Need to keep my investment nice and tidy. Let ol' Jenkins take care of everything..."

His voice fades as Eve spirals back down into oblivion. But his last words echo, a chilling promise: This is only the beginning of how he intends to take care of her.

Hours pass, maybe a day. Eve has no idea. She drifts slowly up through the fog of forced unconsciousness. The potent sedatives Jenkins administered leave her limbs leaden, mind clouded. She clings to the last shreds of oblivion before something collides with her ribcage.

"Wake up, princess!"

Eve's eyes drag open to find Jenkins leering above her, his steel-toed boot poised for another crushing kick. She tries to form words through the chemical haze, but her tongue is a numb weight in her mouth.

Jenkins barks out a sadistic laugh. "What's wrong, cat got your tongue?"

He lashes out again, his boot connecting with her torso. Ribs creak and pop under the force. Agony lances through Eve, but the drugs mute her cries to pitiful mewls.

"On your feet," Jenkins orders, wrenching Eve up by her hair and ignoring her garbled pleas. He shoves a grimy bucket at her, soapy water slopping over to soak the dirty floorboards. "Get scrubbing."

Eve sways unsteadily, narrowed vision dimming at the edges as Jenkins braces his palm against her throat, squeezing. "Best hurry if you know what's good for you… this place isn't gonna clean itself."

He releases his choking grip and Eve crumples to her knees with a weak cough. The filthy brush trembles in her fist as she scrubs at dirt and grime, every movement pure torture. Jenkins towers behind her, promising darker pain to come between each labored swipe if she dares to slow her pace.

Focus fraying, Eve clings to visions of turning the tables, of

Jenkins helpless and screaming beneath her knife one day. She scrubs feverishly, vowing to herself: *I will never be this weak again. However long it takes, I will fucking kill him.*

"Keep scrubbing, girl," Jenkins snarls, dumping another grimy bucket of gray water at Eve's feet.

Though exhaustion weighs on Eve's body and mind from dehydration and the lack of food, she kneels obediently on the warped planks. As she scrubs the first board, the stiff bristles scrape loose all manner of debris — cigarette butts, desiccated insect husks, clumps of dark soil.

Jenkins watches from the musty sofa across the dim cabin, gulping whiskey from a clouded bottle. The liquor only seems to fuel his simmering rage.

Eve lifts her tired eyes from the mindless task. "So how long have you lived out here?" she asks conversationally, as if inquiring about the weather.

Jenkins's lip curls in a reflexive scowl, unappreciative of his captive's initiating idle chatter. "Never you mind about that," he growls. "Put your head down and finish up."

But Eve continues probing him gently between scrubs and brushes across the floorboards, stripping away years of caked filth. "It must get very lonely though, doesn't it? I know if I was isolated out here this long, I'd surely start going half mad from lack of human company."

At this, Jenkins slams his bottle down, splashing whiskey across the worn wooden table. "I said quiet!" he bellows. "Speak again without my permission and you'll regret it, princess."

Eve gives a small nod and resumes scrubbing the filthy floors in silence. Her eyes track Jenkins as he paces the cabin, muttering under his breath. She strains to hear his words.

"Oh Edna," he croons. "If only—"

13

Scott trudges up the steps to his dark, empty house. It's been four days since Eve vanished, and the investigation has stalled. No additional security footage, no witnesses who saw anything useful. Just Eve's purse and phone abandoned in her grocery cart, offering no clues.

Scott sinks onto the couch, head in hands. Each day without answers is agony. He'd spoken with Eve's sister Lucy, her friend Nina, even briefly with some therapist, Dr. Walker, which Scott hadn't actually known Eve had. But none know where she could be.

The house creaks and settles around Scott in the silence. Photos of their smiling wedding day mock him from the mantel. He should be here with his new wife, building their life together. Instead, he's alone with his spiraling thoughts.

A soft knock at the door startles him. He peers out to see a group of familiar faces—his aunt and uncle, as well as neighbors, bearing candles and homemade signs reading "Bring Eve Home."

"We're headed downtown for the vigil," Becky says gently, her eyes brimming with concern. "Thought you might want to join."

Scott's throat tightens. He's touched by his aunt's compassion, but being around people right now feels unbearable.

"I appreciate it," he says. "But I think I need to be alone tonight."

His uncle steps forward. "It won't look good if you don't attend your wife's vigil, Scottie," he says, very much sounding like a lawyer through and through.

Becky looks increasingly concerned but pats his arm. "We understand, dear. But let us know if you need anything."

Scott forces a smile. "Aside from my missing wife back, safe and sound? Nah, I'm fantastic."

His uncle glares at him. "Scott—"

"They've already held two vigils," Scott says. "How many more can they possibly do?"

At that, Aunt Becky looks like she wants to break down in tears, her eyes glistening. His uncle looks like he wants to take off his belt and give Scott a good lashing like he had when he was a kid.

Seeing Becky's reaction, Scott tries to recover. "I mean, Eve would hate all this attention," he says, knowing it's a lie the moment the words slip off his tongue. "There are more important things people could be doing besides standing outside holding a candle—"

"Like what?" his uncle counters.

"Like search and rescue or manning the phones…"

"It's after dark," his uncle says. "Too late for combing fields. And the phones are being manned, you know that."

"It's important we keep her top of everyone's minds," Becky says gently, dabbing her eyes with a tissue. "The vigil will help."

Scott feels a twinge of guilt. "Give me a minute to grab my jacket," he mutters, closing the door.

Scott watches them shuffle down the walk, a procession of flickering lights. He doesn't want to do this. But he knows his uncle is right. And so he goes.

Later, in the dead of night, Scott startles awake to the shrill ring of his cellphone. Still groggy, he fumbles for it in the dark and answers without checking the caller ID.

"Hello?" he croaks.

"Scott? It's me."

He jolts upright. "Eve?"

A chilling laugh answers him. "Nah, just messing with you."

Scott's stomach drops as he realizes it's just a cruel prank call. He slams the phone down, hands shaking. *Motherfuckers.*

Afterward, he lies there, tossing and turning, but mostly staring at the ceiling.

At dawn, a tentative knock at the door interrupts his outrage. Scott drags himself up and is surprised to see Reed's familiar face.

"Sorry to bother you this early," Reed says. "Just wanted to check in, see how you're holding up."

Scott shrugs listlessly. He knows what his friend is really saying. Reed feels bad about the way the two of them left things. "Not too great, to be honest. These fucking people—crank calling me all night, pretending to be Eve…"

Reed rubs the back of his neck, looking uncomfortable. "I know you're convinced Eve was taken, but in cases with newlyweds...sometimes the wife just needs space. Gets overwhelmed with the adjustment and takes off for a bit to clear her head."

Scott's jaw tightens, hands balling into fists. "You think my wife would abandon me like this? That she'd put me through this hell, for what? Fun? Punishment?"

Reed clasps Scott's shoulder sympathetically. "Look, I know you're convinced Eve was taken, but from experience, these missing bride cases often end up being cold feet. The adjustment to married life overwhelms them and they take off for a few days to clear their head, teach their man a lesson."

He shrugs. "I'm not saying that's what happened. But you've gotta consider the possibility your girl just needs time to cool off and will turn up any day now, tail between her legs. As an investigator, I've seen it play out that way more often than not."

Reed squeezes his shoulder. "I'm not discounting foul play here. Just saying we can't ignore the fact that newlyweds sometimes act out of character under the stress. Don't lose hope yet that this is just a lover's quarrel. Eve could waltz through that door tomorrow, ready to kiss and make up."

Scott's jaw tightens. He knows in his gut something terrible is behind Eve's disappearance, regardless of what this small-town, small-minded deputy thinks.

Scott stares at Reed, his friend's words igniting a flame of indignation within him. His voice rises, and the intensity in his eyes is unmistakable. Maybe it's the lack of sleep, maybe it's everything building up to the inevitable. "Eve isn't playing games. Something's happened to her."

"But man, you hardly even know her—have you considered *that*—that maybe it's not everyone else who's wrong?"

Scott steps forward and takes a swing at Reed, the blow landing right at the bridge of his nose. "No."

He looks at his friend lying on the floor and shakes his head in disgust. "Now get out of my house and go do your fucking job."

14

As she scrubs the cabin, Eve logs details of Jenkins endearments, analyzing each reaction, every facial tick and outburst for insight into this unraveling psyche. What wounds might she press to gain the upper hand?

"You missed a spot," Jenkins barks, pointing at the floor. Eve clenches her jaw but forces an appeasing smile.

"My apologies," she says and redirects the bristled brush. Jenkins watches her before retreating over to the sofa, still lost in conversation, still cooing Edna's name.

In his distraction, Eve's smile vanishes. Her thoughts race, probing for flaws to exploit later. She imagines driving him into a rage at the critical moment. Discovering some past conflict that will make him hesitate just long enough for her to run.

As Jenkins watches his ancient sitcoms, Eve probes with more questions. Through news on the TV, Eve learns she has been here for weeks. When Eve asks about the date, or makes any mention of time passing, Jenkins dismisses her. He has ordered her not to speak, but Eve can't help herself. At first, Jenkins only responds to her small defiant acts with verbal threats, seemingly unwilling to damage his new "companion." But with each question, Eve can feel herself inching closer toward that dangerous line, feeling out where it lies. She grows emboldened by what remains unpunished so far, but how much further can she press him?

She longs to ask about the woman in the shed but thinks better of it. For now, Eve resumes her diligent scrubbing and waits.

But later that evening, Jenkins demands that Eve cook a miserable dinner with the rotten vegetables and rancid mystery meat he dumps onto the counter. As she grimaces down at the disgusting ingredients, Eve remarks a little too breezily, "Would it kill you to get some halfway fresh groceries in this place? I will not be very good company if I contract violent food poisoning or botulism…"

The brief flare of unbridled rage in Jenkins's eyes is her only warning before the heavy iron skillet collides with the side of Eve's head, splitting the skin of her temple open.

Crying out in pain and shock, Eve collapses onto the stained floorboards. But Jenkins doesn't stop there. He rains down blows with his meaty fists, pummeling Eve's head over and over as she curls into a ball, trying in vain to protect herself.

Jenkins only ceases when he is panting and exhausted, his knuckles slick with Eve's blood. He looms over her prone body, his face contorted into a horrific mask of fury. "Learn your place here, princess, before I'm forced to teach you again," he spits. "The hard way."

With that, he callously kicks aside her crumpled form as if it were nothing more than a dead animal carcass before storming out of the cabin, locking the door behind him.

Though the small room spins, tilting and shifting around her, Eve grits her teeth and forces herself to sit upright. She scoots back until she can lean against the wall for support. Hands trembling, she begins tentatively exploring the throbbing head wound, wiping away the blood still oozing from it.

The gash feels sizable under her trembling fingers, but the

bleeding seems to slow. Pressing carefully around the torn flesh confirms the injury is not as bad as she feared. Eve releases a shaky breath.

As the adrenaline spike in her veins dissipates, Eve feels a small spark of twisted satisfaction kindling inside her heaving chest. The punishment for her insolence had no doubt been harsh. Even cruel.

But she had goaded Jenkins into striking out. She had crossed the line deliberately, probing for his limits. And now she understood him, and his capacity for brutality, just a bit better. It was all reconnaissance—each piece of information bringing her closer to when she would turn the tables.

Eve probes at the throbbing gash on her temple once more. The bleeding has slowed, but vivid crimson still trickles down her pale cheek. She clenches her teeth as her vision blurs.

Perhaps the head injury is worse than she first assessed. Eve wavers where she sits propped against the cabin wall, her equilibrium thrown.

As the room tilts around her, Eve fights to retain consciousness. Darkness gnaws at the edges of her sight. She sways, no longer able to hold herself upright.

With a weak cry, Eve slumps sideways onto the much cleaner floorboards. Shadows swarm her fading sight like a locust plague.

Just before the light winks out completely, Eve glimpses a pair of sturdy work boots entering her narrowing field of view. The toe of one boot comes to rest right beside her nose.

Jenkins has returned.

Eve struggles to lift her leaden head, to scoot herself away from the looming threat. But it's no use. Her limbs are useless, disconnected things she can no longer command.

Jenkins crouches next to Eve. She tenses as he leans in close.

"Sweet dreams, princess," comes his taunting whisper. She feels the prick of the needle and then he pats her thigh.

"You thought I'd forget...but ol' Jenkins never forgets..."

Eve's eyes flutter a few times before she succumbs fully to the encroaching darkness. She spirals down into its fathomless depths, Jenkins's bitter laughter chasing her all the way down.

15

Jenkins drags Eve across the weed-choked gravel, his calloused fingers clamped around her biceps. The shed looms ahead, a rotting wooden box under a swollen moon.

Eve's pulse thrums. Not again. Eve both craves and dreads showers. Sometimes Jenkins watches, sometimes he doesn't. Sometimes he does other—worse—things.

The rusted door creaks open. The dank air seizes Eve's breath, a moldering stew of mildew, urine and worse. She swallows bile as Jenkins shoves her inside.

"Make it quick." His tobacco-stained sneer twists in the shadows. "Got plans for you tonight."

The door slams shut, a bolt scraping into place.

Eve presses her hands to the wall, gulping air. She inches toward the shower, bracing herself for the icy cold water.

A thin, reedy voice drifts from the vent: "He must like you," she says. "He lets you shower more than the others."

Eve whips around. A pair of pale eyes stare back—wary, yet defiant.

The last few times Eve has showered, her questions have been met with silence. "You're there?"

A rusty chuckle and then she comes into full view, removing the vent cover, poking her head through. "For now."

Eve blinks at the woman's ghastly pallor and her lank blonde hair. *My God.* "What do you mean the others?"

"His other victims. They've all disappeared. It's just me... or it was." She sighs. "Anyway, I thought you were dead." The woman extends a skeletal hand. "He's been so moody lately..."

Eve grasps the woman's icy fingers. "Mira? Right?"

At the woman's nod, the questions spill out in a frenzy. "Oh God, I have so much to ask, not enough time... What happens when he lets you out of this shed? Where does he take you?"

"The main house mostly. He alternates keeping us in the main house, this shed, or the cabin. He never lets us get comfortable. It will be the same for you..." Mira coughs harshly. "Sometimes though, he takes me to the woods."

Eve's pulse picks up. "The woods?"

Mira stares back blankly. "You're still so new..."

"What happens in the woods?"

"He ties me to a tree."

Eve gasps. "For how long?"

"Depends, sometimes an afternoon— sometimes days..."

"Days?"

"Listen—" Mira's lips twist. "I'm sick, and I'm pretty sure he's going to kill me soon. Remember this—*please*—my name is Mira. Mira Adler. I was—I *am*—a teacher. Mason... that's my fiancé's name. If you make it out of here—tell him—tell Mason—I love him." She eyes the gash on Eve's head. "And my parents. Tell them too." Mira's voice cracks. "Okay?"

Eve swallows the bile rising in her throat. "Of course."

A spark glimmers in Mira's eyes. "Hey, do you recall the date when you were taken?"

"November thirteenth."

Tears well in her eyes. "It's been eight months," she says. "I've been here eight months..."

The young woman starts sobbing uncontrollably. "No one ever lasts longer than eight months."

Eve does the math in her head.

Mira sniffles. "Eight is his lucky number."

Eve squeezes Mira's hand, attempting to console her. "Not you. He won't kill you. We'll figure something out."

Mira looks up at Eve then, anger washing over her features. "You have no idea—"

Eve's heart leaps into her throat at the bang of the cellar door.

Jenkins storms in, snarling, "What's taking so long? You think I don't know you've been gossiping with your new friend?"

He wrenches the shower curtain open. Eve shrinks back, water sloshing around her ankles. Mira shrinks through the vent, eyes huge with terror.

Jenkins steps closer, raising his knife. Eve's mind whirls.

"Well?" Jenkins hisses. "Haven't you got anything to say for yourself before I carve out that sly tongue of yours?"

"You're right. I have been gossiping." Eve takes a deep breath. "I just wanted to know why she's still alive."

Jenkins blinks, thrown. The knife wavers. Eve jumps on the opportunity her question has afforded. The words spill out in a nervous jumble. "The others only lasted a few weeks. But Mira's been here for months. Why haven't you killed her yet?"

Just for an instant, a shadow crosses Jenkins's face—confusion? Guilt?

In that fleeting moment, Eve glimpses the truth. Her eyes meet Mira's, a dawning realization in them—

Jenkins's blade flashes toward Eve as she desperately tries twisting away. Searing pain erupts in her foot. Her own screams mingle with Mira's, echoing through the darkness.

Everything descends into chaos.

16

Lucy sits curled on the lumpy hotel bed, nursing a glass of crappy wine she picked up from the convenience store down the street. She doesn't know what her sister ever saw in this town. It isn't charming; it doesn't even have a hotel good enough to come with the simplest of amenities: a mini bar.

The small TV mounted to the wall plays muted infomercials in the background as she halfheartedly scrolls social media on her phone, hoping for any shred of news about her missing sister. She searches local hashtags and locations, desperate for updates. Being in this depressing town feels surreal.

She's relieved when her phone finally rings, grateful for the distraction. But the number is blocked. Lucy hesitates before answering.

"Hello?"

Only silence greets her. She repeats the greeting, firmer this time. Still nothing.

"Hello?" she demands, sitting up straighter. She can hear raspy breathing on the other end of the line. "Okay, I'm hanging up.."

After a few tense beats, a distorted voice responds. "Do you miss your sister?"

Lucy inhales sharply, nearly dropping the phone. Every hair on her body stands on end.

"Where is she?" Lucy hisses into the receiver. "What have you done with Eve? "

The garbled voice chuckles darkly. "Maybe you'll find out soon enough."

The call ends abruptly. Lucy stares wild-eyed at the phone, hands trembling, unsure if she should scream or break something. Was that real or some kind of sick prank? Should she call her dad? The police?

Before she can decide her next move, another call comes through. Lucy answers immediately.

"Hello? Please, tell me what you've done with my sister!" Her throat aches, on the verge of tears. "We can pay—whatever you want—"

"Lucy? It's Mom. Are you all right, honey? You sound upset."

Lucy exhales loudly. "Mom. Sorry, I... I thought you were someone else."

"Who, dear?" Her mother's question comes out robotically, no real concern in her tone.

Lucy rubs her temples, head throbbing. She pours herself another brimming glass of wine. If her mother knew how much Lucy was drinking, she'd only worry what the neighbors might think.

"It was...I don't know…just some stupid prank call about Eve." Her mother has never understood Eve, or their sisterly bond.

"You don't sound like yourself, honey…" Her mother repeats the expected platitudes, though her words lack comfort or care.

"I guess I'm on edge, being here, waiting for answers."

"Oh, sweetie. Any updates yet?"

Lucy's chin quivers. She takes a long swig of wine to steady her nerves. She knows her mother is too preoccupied with her garden and with shopping and her friends to be in *any* way connected to what is *really* going on. She loves her daughters, sure. But not like a mother should. "No. And I'm really starting to think I shouldn't have come. This town is *nothing* like Eve said. It's actually kind of creepy..."

"Creepy?" Judgment creeps into her mother's voice. "What do you mean, creepy?"

Lucy scrambles to justify herself, knowing her mother will pounce on any excuse to criticize. "I don't know—like in a *Stepford Wives* kind of way. If—the Stepford wives were lower middle class, I mean..."

"I don't recall them being wealthy in the movie, do you?"

Lucy pinches the bridge of her nose. It's typical, her mother being worried about a minor movie detail than her own missing daughter. "It's a book, Mom."

"Okay—" There's a long beat of silence. "So, listen, honey, I can't say I'm seeing your point here—but—um, oh, have you been drinking?"

"Me?" Lucy lets out a long, heavy sigh. Her mother with the constant nagging. On second thought, she can almost see why her sister would run as far away as she could, even if it was to a town like this. "I'm just tired. I told you that!"

"Oh, Luc—your father and I told you not to go down there, honey. Daddy has hired the *best* investigators, men with *actual* experience. You know that..."

"No," Lucy shakes her head. "I mean, I know, Mom. But she's my *sister*. I know Eve better than anyone. I guess I just wanted to see for myself."

"Well, now you've seen. I'll have your father charter a flight straightaway. Get you out of there."

"I'm going to the house. I want to see it before I go."

"Oh, honey. Don't. You know we tried to tell Evie, but she wouldn't listen. I have a feeling that man is dangerous, and I couldn't bear it if something happened to you, too."

"Nothing's going to happen, Mom. I'm not Eve."

"I know you're not, sweetie." Her mother sighs, either understanding her youngest daughter has no intention of heeding her warning, or not caring. It's hard to say which. "Listen, I gotta go, but I'm going to have Dad give you a ring in a few. He'll set your mind right about everything."

"My sister is missing—your *daughter* is missing. There's nothing that could set my mind right."

"Oh, Lucy. You know that's not what I meant. I love you. You'll call if you hear anything?"

"I'll call."

17

Lucy grimaces as she pulls up outside the rundown house her sister had purchased with Scott. She shouldn't be shocked, but she is. Eve always did have terrible taste in men. How someone like her found herself stuck in dreary Oak Hollow playing house with a cowboy wannabe should not have been a big mystery, and yet it was. It really was. To everyone.

A chill walks up Lucy's spine. This is way worse than she thought. The place is straight out of a horror movie—overgrown weeds, peeling paint, creaky steps leading to the tiny porch. Hardly the life Eve grew up in. Their father had built an empire; Eve wanted for nothing. Yet here she was, slumming it with a man like Scott in small-town squalor.

Lucy raps sharply on the front door, one of the few things to have been updated in the last half century. Scott answers, worn ball cap shading his eyes. Lucy waits for him to invite her in, but he simply props the storm door open with his boot.

"Well? Aren't you going to ask me in?" Lucy says impatiently.

Scott rubs his stubble and then shrugs. "Sure."

Lucy bristles at his nonchalant tone. She steps inside, wrinkling her nose at the lingering stench of sawdust.

“I had a disturbing prank call just now,” she says. “Thought you should know, in case it's related to Eve's disappearance somehow."

Scott's jaw tightens, accentuating his sharp features. “What did they say?”

Lucy recounts the cryptic call, studying Scott’s reaction. But his expression remains stoic.

"Could be a lead. Or just some sicko," he says. “I’ll mention it to the deputy.”

He may put on a tough exterior, but Lucy senses Scott’s worry, or guilt, about Eve simmering underneath. Even if he doesn’t have anything to do with Eve’s disappearance, Lucy knows for sure that she will always blame him. Her sister never would’ve ended up in peril if not for marrying this loser.

Lucy paces the living room, her heels clicking against the raw wooden floor. She glances at the walls, half stripped of wallpaper, the mess of tools and paint cans strewn about. Scott leans against the door frame to the kitchen, arms crossed over his chest.

"You're renovating this place yourself?" Lucy asks, skepticism lacing her tone. The words sound foreign coming from her mouth, and even she isn’t quite sure why she says them, why it matters.

Scott nods, a flicker of pride in his eyes. "With Eve. I mean, we have help. But it was supposed to be our project."

Lucy snorts, circling a dubious finger in the air. "Some project."

He ignores her jab, moving to pick up a photo frame from a dusty side table. It's a picture of him and Eve, both smiling with paint on their faces. "She was happy here, you know."

Lucy whirls on him, her gaze icy. She isn’t sure whether he means in the photo or in general. Either way, this is her chance to shoot her shot, to tell him what she really thinks. “Happy?” she scoffs. “Scott, she was abducted from a grocery store parking lot. This"—she waves a hand at their surroundings—"isn't happiness; it's purgatory. It shows you don’t know my sister at all.”

Scott sets the frame down harder than necessary. "That's not fair. You have no idea—"

"Don't I?" Lucy interrupts. "I know my sister better than anyone." She steps closer to him until they're almost nose to nose. "Clearly better than you."

He matches her intensity, not backing down an inch. "If you knew her so well, why didn't you see how much she needed this?"

"Needed what?"

"Coming here." He shrugs. "She wanted a fresh start."

"A fresh start?" Lucy throws her hands up in exasperation. "More like an escape."

Scott's face darkens; he takes a step toward Lucy as if he's about to say something harsh but stops himself.

Lucy scoffs and moves away from him, looking around the house with disdain.

"Was it you behind the plane ticket to Hawaii?" he challenges.

Lucy whirls back to face him, her eyes narrowing. "Me? She was coming back to herself! Trying to remember who she was before...before all this!"

"All this?" Scott's voice cracks with emotion as he gestures around them. "This is what she wanted—"

Lucy shakes her head vehemently. "You can't see it because you don't want to! She was lost here and now she's gone!"

Silence hangs between them for a moment before Scott speaks again.

"You think I don't blame myself every second of every day? That I don't lie awake at night wondering if this is all my fault?" His voice breaks with barely suppressed anger and sorrow.

Lucy takes a step back, taken aback by his raw emotion, but not deterred.

"You should have protected her," she spits out.

"And you should have supported her!" Scott retorts.

The tension is palpable; they stand staring at each other as if seeing each other clearly for the first time—two people who love Eve in their own ways.

Lucy scrutinizes Scott in the dim entryway, searching for any break in his stony composure. But his sharp features remain etched in hard lines, jaw tense.

"A loving husband would be breaking down doors to find his missing wife," Lucy says, unable to restrain her swirling judgment.

Scott meets her glare, defiance flashing. "You think I'm not doing everything I can? Questioning me won't help Eve, Lucy."

Lucy looks away. Deep down, she knows Scott is right, that her bitterness solves nothing. But her stubborn pride and a whole lot of resentment simmers inside just the same. Eve might be halfway around the world on a beach right now if not for Scott tying her down, keeping her here, even though he could see she was desperately missing home.

An engine roar outside shatters the tense silence. Lucy moves toward the window, and though she isn't sure why, her pulse quickens. Through the half-open blinds, she spots a dark truck idling at the end of Scott's driveway like a prowling animal.

"Do you know that truck?" Lucy asks.

Scott crowds beside her at the window, arm brushing hers. Lucy expects him to deny any connection, but instead his face drains of color. He moves for the front door without answering her.

"Scott?" Lucy calls in confusion as he disappears outside. She hesitates, then dashes out after him into the deepening dusk. But Scott is already halfway down the overgrown drive, confronting the shadowy figure at the idling truck's door...

18

Scott charged toward the truck, rage propelling his long strides. He wrenched open the driver's side door before Levi could react.

"What the hell?" Levi threw his hands up in surprise.

Scott's fist closed around a handful of Levi's shirt. With a sharp jerk, he hauled the smaller man from the truck, throwing him against the side panel.

"You son of a bitch," Scott growled through gritted teeth. "Morris put you up to smearing Eve's name?"

"Whoa, take it easy!" Levi's face drained of color. "I was just doing my job—"

The excuse sent Scott over the edge. He pulled back and smashed his fist into Levi's nose. Cartilage crunched under his knuckles. Blood spurted as Levi howled in pain, hands flying to his face.

Scott barely felt the sting blooming across his skinned knuckles. Rage consumed him, narrowing his vision to the weasel of a man cringing before him.

"Please, man—stop!" Levi blubbered through the gush of red running over his lips.

Scott cocked back again for another blow but hesitated. Pummeling Levi might provide some fleeting satisfaction, but it wouldn't bring Eve back. He lowered his fist as Levi sank to the ground with a whimper, fumbling for a handkerchief.

Breathing hard, Scott paced a tight circle, dragging a hand through his hair. That piece of trash Morris just wanted to save his own skin. Pin it on Eve being some runaway socialite instead of admitting his department was incompetent and that this town might not actually be as perfect or as safe as everyone thinks. Scott spit on the dirt. He'd known Morris was useless from the start, but never imagined his corruption ran this deep.

He wasn't exactly surprised. Still, this changed everything. He was on his own finding Eve. No backup or resources from anyone in this town, just a man possessed with nothing left to lose. He turned back to Levi, still huddled by the rear tire. Kneeling, Scott fisted the man's shirt collar until their noses nearly touched, Levi's blood dripping between them.

"I'm only going to tell you this once," Scott said, his voice low and lethal. "Print one more worthless word about my wife, and your editor will be publishing your obituary next. Are we clear?"

Levi gave a frantic nod, eyes rounded in fear. With another shove, Scott flung the man sideways and rose to his feet. As an afterthought, he kicked the truck's rear panel, putting a sizable dent in the metal. Minor damage, but it gave him a rush of satisfaction. Let Levi explain that to his boss.

Scott glanced back at the house. Lucy stood on the porch, phone held aloft, blatantly filming the entire incident. Scott dismissed her with a wave. He didn't care what she did with the footage.

Although he should have. He really should have.

19

Eve grits her teeth as she scrubs at the floor of the main house, agony pulsing through her bandaged foot. Jenkins had stabbed her there in his last violent outburst, punishment for talking with Mira.

Jenkins says she has to clean at night on account of Edna, so he keeps Eve awake at all hours, forcing her to survive on little sleep, unless she's heavily drugged, which she often is.

Eve hums defiantly, despite the pain, taking petty pleasure in this act of rebellion. Jenkins despises anything that makes her seem human, but she clings to these subtle, defiant acts. They're all she has left now.

Her brief alliance with Mira had ended abruptly that night. After Jenkins attacked, he'd locked Eve in the cabin for days without tending to her injury. By the time Jenkins returned, there was no sign of Mira, only a dark stain Eve fears is blood remains where Mira had been huddled that night, the vent now sealed shut.

Eve tortures herself with the possibilities—did she get Mira killed with her prying? Is he keeping her elsewhere? But Jenkins only smiles coldly when Eve asks after Mira, taunting her with the not knowing, using the mystery to deepen her agony.

The bucket sloshes as Eve dips her rag in, the pungent scent of bleach stinging her eyes. Her knuckles whiten around the handle, the familiar tune she's humming under her breath the only thing keeping her tethered to sanity.

The floorboards creak, heralding Jenkins's approach. Eve braces herself, scrubbing aggressively despite the fiery pain pulsing through her injured foot. She glances up belligerently as Jenkins stops beside her, meeting his suspicious stare. She's being punished, and still, she's testing him.

"What's that racket?" His pale eyes narrow, scanning the room. Searching for a reason to unleash his rage.

She shrugs, feigning nonchalance. "Just cleaning like you asked."

The floorboards groan under his weight as he stalks toward her, each step slow and deliberate. "You're lying. I know what you're doing."

Her fingers tighten around the rag, her knuckles screaming. She forces her lips into a mocking smile, the split in her bottom lip stinging. "And what would that be?"

He grabs a fistful of her hair, yanking her head back so hard her neck cracks. She gasps, pain lancing through her skull, but she doesn't drop her gaze.

Let him see she's not afraid.

His face contorts, fury etched into every crease. "You think I don't know that song? You think I don't know what you're trying to do?" Spittle flies from his lips, flecking her cheeks. "You'll never escape. You're mine, you hear me?"

Her scalp burns, her eyes watering, but she grins up at him. "Why would I ever want to leave?"

With a roar, he hurls her across the room. She crashes into the wall, crumpling to the floor in a tangle of limbs.

Before she can suck in a breath, he's dragging her up by her hair again, toward the shed where, if she doesn't act fast, her screams will soon echo into the night.

She digs her heels in, scrambling for purchase on the packed dirt. Her foot throbs, but she ignores the pain. *No. Oh God, no, not the shed again.*

Panic rises in her chest, but she beats it back down.

He yanks harder, snarling like an animal, spittle flying from his lips. "Think you're so clever, don't you? I'll show you what happens to clever girls like you, princess."

The shed looms before them, a crumbling monument to madness and death. Bile rises in her throat, but she swallows it down, refusing to show fear. With a roar, he hurls her through the doorway of the shed. She crashes to the floor, agony exploding through her shoulder.

Before she can move, the door slams shut, plunging her into darkness. The rasp of a lock clicks into place.

Oh, god. No. Panic swells in her chest, strangling her. Not the dark, not again—

She scrambles to her feet, ignoring the pain shrieking through her foot, and hurls herself at the door.

"Let me out! You bastard, let me out!" She pounds on the wood, splinters digging into her bunched fists, as the darkness presses in around her.

Laughter drifts through the walls, underlaid with madness. “It's time for your treatment, you know that…”

She pounds the rough planks, screaming into oblivion. Only muffled laughter answers her raw cries.

The door creaks open, and moonlight spears Eve's eyes. She cowers as Jenkins's hulking shape crosses the threshold, towing strange equipment. Copper bowls suspended from wires. Tubes and tanks of bubbling liquids.

“Time for your treatment,” his raspy voice singsongs.

Eve scrambles back, but Jenkins is faster. His giant hand clamps her thrashing arm, while the other produces a syringe. Eve bucks wildly as the needle's sting blooms, forcing vile fluid into her veins.

The shed tilts, Jenkins's pockmarked face swimming. His grinning mouth moves, but the words glug strangely. Eve's limbs turn to stone, the cold bite of metal disks pressed to her temples, barely registering through numbness.

She strains against paralysis, watching Jenkins fiddle with his witchcraft paraphernalia. The wire contraption lowers toward Eve's head. Jenkins's feverish eyes glint behind it.

"You'll feel much better soon..."

His warped promise fades as chemical darkness engulfs Eve's mind.

She jolts awake later, alone. Jenkins's torture devices stand silent. The door hangs open, moonlight mocking the escape.

A trap. Of course, it's a trap.

Her heart jackhammers against her ribs as she presses into the corner, the walls undulating. Sickly sweet drug aftertaste coats her tongue. She blinks against double vision—no sign of Jenkins.

But she knows he's in here. Watching. Waiting.

The walls continue to tilt and sway as panic rises in her throat, blackness swirling before her eyes. She can't breathe, can't see, can't escape—

She drags in a slow, shaky breath, clenching her hands into fists. He wants her to panic. Wants her to break.

She won't give him the satisfaction.

The floorboards creak again, and she tenses, bracing herself.

The air shifts behind her. She whirls around, lashing out. Her fingernails rake across Jenkins' face as he crouches on the floor, finding purchase in the soft, vulnerable flesh of his eye. A grunt of pain, and Jenkins recoils, pressing his hands to his face.

Scrambling back, she sees him sprawled out on the floor, writhing in agony.

Did she really—? No time. She lunges for the door, yanking at the lock with bleeding fingers until it gives.

Freedom.

Cold air smacks Eve's face as she staggers outside. The moonlit woods tilt around her. She runs through delirium, bare feet snagging on roots and stones. Branches whip her face as she runs blindly, veering between the trees. Waiting for that mad laughter to echo through the forest.

But there is only silence behind her. No heavy footsteps crashing through the underbrush. No enraged shouts tearing through the night air.

Glancing back, she stumbles over a root, pain lancing through her bandaged foot. *Nothing. No one.*

Each agonized step sends fire through her injured foot, but Eve doesn't dare stop. Adrenaline fuels her frantic escape, bare feet slapping the ground despite the pain.

she runs on, bare feet stinging against twigs and stones. Each gasping breath rakes her throat like shards of glass. She veers wildly, not caring where the woods take her as long as it's far from that wretched shed.

Far from him.

When her legs finally give out, she collapses to her knees in a small clearing. Gulping air, she peers back the way she came. The woods are still and quiet around her. Too quiet.

He should have come after her by now. She presses trembling hands over her mouth to stifle the panicked sobs trying to claw their way out.

It's a trap. It has to be. He's letting her think she escaped, letting her wear herself out. Any moment now, he'll come roaring from the shadows to drag her back.

Eve squeezes her eyes shut, body coiled tight. She waits, her heart caught in her throat, for the meaty hand clamping down on her shoulder or the cold barrel of a shotgun against her neck.

But nothing happens. No sign of her captor in the moonwashed clearing. The forest is empty around her.

Or so it seems...

20

Scott sits hunched on the back porch as dawn creeps across the yard, a half-empty bottle dangling from his fingers. He hasn't slept in days, remorse and fury warring within him.

If only he'd gone to the store himself after work that day instead of sending Eve and then losing track of time at the office. She'd still be here, safe in his arms.

But no—he's failed her. And now the whole town whispers he's a deadbeat loser, just like his old man.

The smart thing to do would be to keep his head down, cooperating with the useless sheriff's department. Instead, he's gone and smashed Levi's face on Lucy's video. Now it's plastered all over the internet and he's looking at assault charges.

Scott drags a hand over his unshaven jaw. He should regret pummeling the little weasel. But oddly, the chaos clears his mind. With Morris compromised, Scott knows finding Eve falls solely on his shoulders. No backup, no resources—just a man past his breaking point.

He takes another burning swig, eyes landing on the ramshackle house—their house. He and Eve have poured blood, sweat and dreams into restoring it together. After years adrift,

Scott has finally found purpose again. And now it's crumbling around him.

The empty bottle slips from Scott's fingers, shattering on the weathered boards. He barely notices, lost in his spiraling thoughts.

An engine rumbles in the distance, growing louder. Headlights cut through the dawn mist creeping over the fields. An unfamiliar truck pulls up the drive, tires spitting gravel.

Scott straightens, pulse kicking. No one comes out here this early unless they're bringing trouble. His hand closes around a rusty tire iron left on the porch.

The truck idles for a long moment before the driver door creaks open. Heavy boots crunch on the gravel drive. Scott's grip tightens on the makeshift weapon, body coiled to spring. Friend or foe, he's ready.

A large silhouette appears out of the mist. Scott squints, dismayed to recognize Deputy Reed's familiar stride—the last person he wants to deal with right now.

"Morning," Reed calls out, neutrally enough. But his hand rests on his holstered sidearm as he approaches.

Scott remains seated, not trusting his temper. "Here to arrest me for assault?"

Reed's mouth quirks. "Not today. Got a tip you might want to hear."

Scott eyes him warily. "What kind of tip?"

"Anonymous call about an abandoned hunting cabin deep in the hollow. Might be worth checking out."

Scott's pulse quickens. A slim lead, but more than they've had. He rises, swaying slightly on unsteady legs.

"Well, what are we waiting for?"

Reed regards him critically. "When's the last time you slept, Collins?"

Scott bristles at the insinuation. "I'm fine. Let's go."

He heads for the truck, ready to tear through the hills if it brings him one step closer to Eve. But Reed's heavy hand lands on his shoulder, halting him.

"Not so fast," Reed cautions, hand firm on Scott's shoulder. "You don't know what we might walk into." His jaw tightens. "You understand, Collins?"

Scott shrugs off Reed's grip, pulse hammering. "So we leave her out there?"

"I didn't say that." Reed scans the dark ridge of trees uneasily. "Truth is, I'm going behind Morris's back here. If this blows up..." He trails off, mouth pressed in a grim line as he meets Scott's eyes. "It'll just be us. I'm not looking to lose my badge."

Scott meets his hard stare. "She's my wife, Reed. I love her. I'd walk into hell to bring her home."

Reed holds his gaze, then nods. "Let's go then. But we watch each other's backs, got it?"

Scott agrees and they climb into Reed's truck, jostling along narrow back roads into the wooded hills. After an hour of driving with no sign of the cabin, frustration mounts.

"Should be around here somewhere," Reed says, peering through the trees.

Another half hour passes before they spot a dilapidated structure tucked among the pines. Pulse quickening, Scott signals Reed to cover him as they pull up. They get out, senses on high alert in the still woods.

Scott eases up the structure's sagging steps with Reed close behind. The battered door hangs off its hinges. Scott nudges it aside with one hand, flashlight in the other, sweeping the dim interior. Just a makeshift deer blind, long abandoned. No tracks or any sign of life.

Scott curses, kicking the weathered door in frustration. Another wasted search.

Reed steps up behind him. "Hey, we'll find her. Could still be a lead if someone's using these cabins as stash points."

Scott scrubs a hand over his face, tamping down despair. As

they head back, he glances over his shoulder at the decaying blind. A perfect spot for hiding something, or someone. The tip couldn't have just been coincidence... could it?

His instincts scream that Eve is out here somewhere, waiting. Scott swears then and there he won't stop searching every inch of the earth until she's safe in his arms again.

As the truck rumbles back down the winding road, he peers out the window, scouring the woods for any hint of life or movement in the shadows. But there is nothing. Nothing but an empty house awaiting him and the suspicious gazes of his entire hometown.

21

Lucy collapsed onto the sagging hotel bed, mascara streaking the pillowcase. Another fruitless day searching for Eve when Scott should be the one out pounding the pavement.

She topped off her wine glass with the bottle she'd drained last night. This whole nightmare brought back stifling memories—the way her father always doted on perfect, precious Eve when they were little. No matter how impressive Lucy's grades and achievements were, Eve effortlessly stole the spotlight with her beauty and charm.

Not anymore. A twisted satisfaction emerged in Lucy seeing Eve's picture plastered on telephone posts, for once painted as the damsel in distress instead of the golden child.

Scott thought he was so high and mighty, the way he'd sneered at Lucy for not "supporting" her sister playing frontier wife out here in Nowheresville. If Scott had really cared, maybe he would have provided the stable home Eve deserved instead of a rotting hovel.

The tears flowed faster as wine greased old wounds. Deep down, a needle of guilt pricked at Lucy. She hadn't suggested the trip to Hawaii to rescue her sister—it was just Lucy's latest petty attempt to show Eve up. And now, thanks to Scott's incompetence, Eve was God-knows-where at the mercy of God-knows-who. The not knowing was eating Lucy alive.

That video of Scott pounding the reporter was her ticket to wrestling control of the search efforts away from that unstable asshole. She just had to keep playing the game smarter than Eve ever could. For once, Lucy would come out on top, overshadowing the perfect Princess Eve at last.

She emptied her wineglass in one long gulp. One way or another, Lucy would find her sister. She'd make damn sure of that. Then, finally, she'd get the acknowledgment she deserved.

22

Eve limps through the shadowy forest, her bandaged foot afire. With every agonizing step, blood seeps through dirty wrappings, the stab wound torn open during flight.

The drugs make her head spin as trees tilt at odd angles around her. She knows her escape was too easy. Any moment, Jenkins will come roaring from the trees to drag her back. So she forces herself onward despite the fiery pain, putting as much distance as she can between herself and that monster.

Each snap of a twig makes her flinch, certain it's the heavy stomp of his boots. But no one emerges. The woods remain eerily silent around her except for her own labored breaths and the pounding of blood in her ears.

As she presses on, a gnawing ache builds in her foot until soon, each step feels like walking on hot coals. Still, she dares not stop. Her only thought is getting farther away, even if she has no idea where she's going.

Eve is driven by pure adrenaline and the instinct to survive. A violent snap explodes the air, metal jaws clamping shut on her ankle with bone-crushing force. The steel trap snares her foot as she crashes hard amid the dried leaves and dirt. Pain whites out the world for a split second, and her screams slice the air.

She lies paralyzed in mossy undergrowth, rusted metal chewing her mangled leg while phantom footsteps circle overhead...

As the initial shock fades to a blinding throb, Eve drags herself upright, clawing at the trap. She has to pry it off, has to keep moving before he finds her.

But the primitive device holds fast, teeth embedded to the bone. Eve collapses back with a sob, unable to wrench it loose. She thrashes about in a panic, which only worsens the pain.

Hot blood flows from the deep punctures in her shredded ankle. The pain is excruciating, but more terrifying is the helplessness—she's pinned here like a butterfly on a card, unable to flee. Easy prey.

Through her anguished cries, Eve hears the heavy tread of boots approaching. She made it farther than she realized, if he's only now catching up. Not that the distance matters anymore.

Jenkins emerges from the trees, lips curled in a sadistic grin as he surveys her predicament.

"Clever girl. But not clever enough."

He crouches beside her, prying open the trap almost casually as Eve whimpers. She lashes out in desperation, but he effortlessly catches her flailing fist in an iron grip.

"None of that now. You're only making this worse for yourself."

Eve shrieks as he releases the trap's jaws from her mangled ankle. The pain is blinding, white hot. She feels the blood draining from her head as her vision starts to narrow.

Jenkins seizes her under the arms and begins dragging her limp body back through the woods. Each small jostle sends fresh agony lancing through Eve's shredded ankle.

She tries to remain conscious, but the pain is too much. As the crumbling outline of the shed comes into view between the trees, darkness creeps into the edges of her sight.

Eve's head lolls back as her eyes roll up, limbs going slack. The last thing she hears before losing her tenuous grip on awareness is Jenkins's taunting voice.

"Sweet dreams, princess."

When Eve comes to, she is inside the cabin, ankle throbbing. She finds herself bound hand and foot, restraints biting into her wrists and calves. Blood still oozes from her injured ankle.

Jenkins looms over her, pale eyes glinting with malicious delight. "Welcome back," he sneers. "You really shouldn't have done that. Edna is going to be so angry."

23

Scott tugs at the chokehold of a tie cinched around his neck as his aunt and uncle exchange last-minute advice.

"Flash those baby blues and really turn on the waterworks," Aunt Becky says, fussing to tuck in Scott's shirt. "Make 'em feel your pain, so they keep this story cooking."

Scott grimaces, but Becky either doesn't notice or care that he loathes performing this tear-soaked, grieving husband routine when Eve is still out there somewhere.

Scott's uncle grips his shoulder, his lined face grave. "I know this circus isn't your style. But keep taking every opportunity to keep Eve's name front and center. It's our best shot at answers."

Scott knows his uncle is right, but that doesn't make facing the cameras easier. He already hated how this small-town rumor mill had been churning about him and Eve before she disappeared. Now the glare of media scrutiny feels equal parts intrusive and inadequate.

Still, as Scott steps toward the buzzing conference room to a chorus of shouted questions, he girds himself. If suffering through vultures picking over the bones of his marriage might shake loose a clue to his missing wife, he can endure a lot worse.

At the podium, Scott clears his throat roughly. "I'm here to repeat my plea for any shred of information about my wife, Eve." His voice wavers before hardening with resolve.

"What makes you so sure your wife even wants to be found?" a reporter shouts out.

Scott's jaw clenches, but he forces composure. He needs to get through this circus.

As the camera flashes pulse faster, he stares straight at their hollow focus. The quicker he sates their salivating headlines, the quicker he can get back to the search.

"Some folks are saying maybe Eve finally got fed up and left. Any response?" another journalist calls out.

Scott's grip tightens on the sides of the podium. "My wife would never just walk away without explanation," he grinds out.

Scott feeds the journalists Eve's description in short, emotionless sentences. His hands grip the sides of the podium under hot lights until his knuckles blanch. This execution via media might uncover a lead. It is the only hope that stops him from smashing cameras and storming away from their intrusive glare.

When he finally utters "That's all for today," the eruption of shouted inquiries nearly pulls a growl from his clenched jaw. Scott turns stiffly, bracing against their cacophony.

As he turns to go, teeth clenched against their assault, a voice rings out over the din.

"Just one more question!"

Scott pauses, inhaling slowly as all eyes fixate on him. He nods sharply for the reporter to continue.

"Do you have anything to hide regarding your wife's disappearance?"

As the cameras explode with flickers at the bold challenge, it takes all of Scott's restraint not to spit venom at these insatiable vultures. Instead he stalks away, their barrage echoing down the hallway.

His hurried exit stirs more rapid-fire camera clicks. Scott

escapes behind the blessed barricade of deputies guarding the conference room entrance. As their insatiable chatter drones on without him, Scott sags against the wall.

If groveling for the public's help fails to bring Eve home soon, his next move will be a private one.

24

Eve awakes to pitch darkness. Disoriented, she blinks around the small room, waiting for her eyes to adjust. The emaciated shape of Brutus, Jenkins's pet possum, draws her wary attention. The creature's bones push through malnourished flesh as he gnaws desperately at the chains barely keeping him from Eve.

The throbbing pain in her head has dulled to a faint ache, though confusion clouds her mind. How long has she been imprisoned here with Brutus, her only company? His beady black eyes follow her every twitch with maddening hunger.

She strains against the ropes binding her hands and feet. There's no slack. Eve sags back resignedly as Brutus gnashes his teeth, struggling in vain against his bonds too.

Eve focuses on steadying her breathing, just as her therapist had taught her during anxiety attacks. But the racing thoughts and panicked tears come anyway. Will she die caged in this wretched cabin, forgotten by the outside world? Will she ever see Scott again? Brutus fixates on Eve, desperate hunger burning in the possum's eyes.

A loud thump at the cabin's front door makes Eve jump before it swings open. Muted daylight floods the front room. Heavy boots cross the creaky floorboards toward where Eve is bound. She squeezes her eyes shut against the blinding light. Jenkins has come to give her antibiotics and treat her ankle.

"Wakey wakey," Jenkins's gravelly voice taunts. Eve shudders as he enters the room and clicks on the small television in the corner, keeping the sound low.

"Thought you might wanna see what your husband's been up to." The way he says "husband" oozes contempt.

Eve squints at the screen as an overhead shot of her neighborhood fills the frame, crowded with news vans and reporters. The caption below reads "Desperate Plea for Missing Woman." Eve's breath catches.

The camera zooms in on Scott, standing before a mountain of microphones, his eyes sunken and clothes disheveled. Her heart breaks seeing him so anguished.

"Please," Scott begs the cameras. "If anyone knows where my wife Eve is, come forward. I need her back safely." His voice cracks. "Don't believe the garbage people are saying about why she left. Eve wouldn't abandon me without a word. Something...something terrible must have happened."

He looks utterly crushed. Eve longs to reach through the screen and comfort him. Anger simmers within her, knowing Jenkins is showing this coverage to torment her.

The news ticker along the bottom of the footage catches Eve's eye: "Missing Woman's Sister Claims Foul Play." The camera cuts to Eve's sister Lucy, issuing a public plea, mascara running down her cheeks. "She wouldn't just leave everything behind. My sister would never do that to our family..."

Eve is encouraged to see her family fighting for her. But she worries what dangers they might be putting themselves in.

As if reading her mind, Jenkins says, "Your sister's a real looker, ain't she?"

The coverage cuts back to the studio anchors analyzing Eve's case. Photos and bank statements of Scott's appear on screen as the male anchor shakes his head in disgust.

"Police sources confirm Mr. Collins is drowning in debt," he says. "Folks are starting to wonder if his wife got fed up playing house with an underemployed failure."

The screen cuts to commercial. Eve stares numbly as Jenkins laughs.

"Can't say I blame you for wanting out, Princess," he chuckles, tramping toward the front door and locking her in darkness. He stops, turns back and tosses a few scraps for Brutus, leaving Eve with nothing. "You're much better off here, where I can take care of you."

Rage and helplessness suffocate her. She thinks of Scott, subjected to baseless accusations while sick with worry for her, and she knows she has to escape this prison by any means necessary...for both their sakes.

25

Lucy sidled up to the dive bar, gravel crunching under her heels. She'd followed Deputy Reed here after his shift ended, to a neon-bathed watering hole miles outside town. Perfect—no prying eyes.

Inside, shc spotted Reed's rugged frame hunched over a whiskey. An opportunity too tempting to resist. She checked her lipstick in a compact mirror and shook out her long blonde hair.

"Well, hey there, Deputy," Lucy purred, occupying the stool beside him. "Fancy running into you here."

Reed straightened, surprise flashing across his craggy features at Lucy's unexpected presence. She watched his guarded eyes sweep over her clingy dress and painted red lips.

"Evening, Miss Burke," he said. "What brings you out this way?"

"Oh, I just needed a change of scenery." She gestured for the bored bartender. "This town is so dreary...and I can't stop seeing my sister's face everywhere I turn..."

As she spoke of Eve, Lucy forced her voice to crack ever so slightly. Right on cue, the deputy's expression softened.

"No breaks in your sister's case yet," Reed offered gently. "But the guys are working real hard tracking down leads."

"I know you're doing everything you can. I just wish I could do more to help." Lucy edged closer as two amber shots arrived. The spicy whiskey burned smoothly down her throat.

As Reed updated her on the investigation, Lucy shifted to expose more bare thigh. His eyes darted to the creamy flesh before reverting back to his drink. Got him.

"Enough shop talk," she sighed, lightly touching his wrist. "Thinking about poor Eve just wears me out. Distract me for a while..."

One strategic tear slipped onto her cheekbone. Reed faltered, visibly warring with being drawn to the vulnerability lurking under Lucy's brilliance. Just one intimate evening—it was all she needed to wrap this backwoods deputy around her manicured finger.

Lucy arched forward, lips parted, ready to seal the deal. Her pulse quickened in anticipation. She had him right where she wanted him.

But just as she moved to close the distance between them, Reed froze. His expression shuttered as he held up a hand. "I can't do this, Miss Burke."

Lucy recoiled. "What do you—"

"I think you best settle your tab and be on your way." Reed's gravelly tone allowed no room for argument. He was already shrugging on his jacket, jaw set.

Before she could respond, he strode out without a backward glance. The remaining patrons eyed Lucy as she sat, stunned. She stared after him, shock shifting to rage, plans crumbling around her. How had he resisted her charms? She was so close to getting what she needed.

By the time the motel sign flickered into view, Lucy's fists were white on the steering wheel. If she'd learned anything from the smug golden child, it was that you didn't always get what you want on the first try. And Lucy wasn't about to let one stubborn man stand between her and success.

26

Eve stifles a gasp as Jenkins steps through the door of the decrepit cabin, his boots caked in mud, Mira's limp body cradled in his arms. The woman is barely recognizable, her hair a matted tangle of knots, eyes sunken into dark hollows. Pale and emaciated, she is little more than skin and bones. He dumps Mira's utterly still form on the floor, but she doesn't move or make a sound.

Eve's heart skips a beat as she takes in the sight before her. She had known, deep down, that Mira's situation would end in devastation, but seeing her in this state feels like a gut punch. How could someone do this? How could a person be responsible for such cruelty?

"W-what have you done to her?" Eve stammers, her voice quivering with a mix of fear and anger.

Jenkins chuckles, a sound that sends shivers crawling up Eve's spine. "Oh, she put up quite a fight," he says, his tone laced with sadistic satisfaction. He retreats back outside briefly, returning with a bag from a drugstore chain. He tosses the sack at her, and first aid supplies tumble out.

Eve recoils on the mattress, her head swimming. She wants to scream, to rush at Jenkins and claw his eyes out. But she knows that would only make things worse. So she forces herself to stay calm, pushing down the fury rising within her.

"Just tell me what you want me to do," she says evenly.

Jenkins sneers. "What I want is for you to fix her up. I went a little too far this time, it seems." He nods at the bag of gauze and antiseptic. "I can't have her dying on me before I'm finished with her. Get to work."

With that, he grabs Brutus and stalks out of the cabin, slamming the door behind him. Eve rushes to Mira's side, gently lifting her head into her lap. Tears blur her vision as she takes in Mira's battered form.

"I've got you," she whispers. "Just hold on."

Swallowing rage, Eve kneels over Mira. She clears matted hair from Mira's cuts as gently as possible, hiding her disgust. The crusted gashes, the finger marks circling Mira's limp wrists, speak to depraved violations.

Eve hastily gathers the kit Jenkins dumped at her feet—bandages, ointments, a needle and thread for stitches. Her hands tremble as she starts cleaning Mira's wounds, working quickly but carefully. But even as she works to save Mira minute by minute, Eve's thoughts turn to revenge...and escape.

Days blur into nights as Eve tends to Mira's injuries, her heart heavy with guilt for contributing to the situation. The cabin is a hellish place, a dank and stifling environment that perpetuates Jenkins's twisted whims. Mira takes baby steps toward recovery each day, her spirit refusing to break even in the face of such cruelty. Eve, too, fights to keep her own fragile sanity intact, the weight of her responsibility bearing down on her like an unyielding storm cloud. She has no idea how much time is passing, only that Mira's cuts are starting to heal.

Mira doesn't speak much; only once does she say anything of substance. "Edna," she mumbles. "Edna is his weakness."

Eve doesn't give it much thought at the time. She's too concerned with trying to keep Mira alive. Not only does she not want her to die, she doesn't trust that Jenkins won't leave her alone with Mira's corpse as punishment. A possum she can nearly tolerate...a rotting body to reminder of her own fate...not so much.

With each passing hour, Eve feels Jenkins lurking, his creeping presence infecting every corner like malevolent shadows stretching the length of their confined space.

She'll look up to find his silhouette filling the doorway, eyes glittering behind alcohol's haze, watching. Eve forces herself not to shudder at the implied warning whenever his heavy boots echo closer across the floorboards.

Eve senses Jenkins cataloging her efforts tending to Mira, sees him studying them with ominous intent. Something in his too-calm demeanor whispers, "it's time for her treatment."

Eve watches warily as Jenkins grabs a syringe and a vial of mysterious fluid. She guesses this is the next phase of his sadistic efforts to dominate her mind and spirit.

He babbles something about this concoction wiping memories clean, making Eve his utterly compliant prisoner. The serum must connect to the strange contraptions he'd forced onto her head previously.

Eve blinks in confusion as Jenkins approaches her, a look of defiance still visible on her face. He raises the syringe, and her eyes glaze over as she feels the needle prick her arm. A wave of dizziness washes over her as the drugs begin to take effect, and her world starts to slip away.

Eve struggles to keep her eyes open as the medication courses through her veins. She sways unsteadily, desperately trying to cling to consciousness, but the cabin spins around her. Jenkins leers down at her, his twisted smile the last thing she sees before the darkness takes over.

When Eve comes to, she finds herself strapped to a chair. Her mind feels foggy, thoughts drifting hazily through a dense cloud. Jenkins leans in close, his rancid breath hot on her face.

"Welcome back," he purrs. "How do you feel?"

Eve blinks slowly, trying to clear the haze from her mind. Where is she? What's happening? She tries to speak, but her tongue feels thick and heavy in her mouth.

Jenkins laughs, a chilling sound that sends a shiver down her spine. "Don't struggle, princess. The serum did its job perfectly. You're mine now, to do with as I please."

He turns, and Eve follows his gaze to Mira's frail form huddled in the corner. Rage boils up inside Eve as Jenkins approaches Mira. She strains against the straps holding her down, willing her sluggish limbs to move, to fight, but it's no use.

Jenkins grabs Mira by the hair and wrenches her head back. Mira cries out in pain, and Eve screams, the sound ripping from her throat. Jenkins glances back at her, amusement dancing in his cruel eyes.

"Oh good, you can still feel something. We'll have to work on that."

He throws Mira aside and stalks back to Eve. Eve braces herself, jaw clenched, as Jenkins leans in close. She may be trapped, but she won't give him the satisfaction of seeing her fear.

Eve stares defiantly into Jenkins's cold eyes, refusing to cower before this monster. Somewhere deep in her clouded mind, a spark of determination still flickers. She will not break.

"My sweet princess," he croons. "You'll learn to appreciate my gentle touch."

"My name is Eve."

Jenkins laughs at her pathetic attempt at courage, and Eve's skin crawls at his sinister amusement. She can practically hear his unspoken thought as he leers—soon enough she will be his plaything, obedient and malleable to whatever sick games his twisted mind conjures.

"I see the serum hasn't fully taken effect. No matter. I have all the time in the world to break you."

He turns back to Mira, who cowers on the floor. Eve strains against her bonds once more, desperate to intervene, but her body betrays her. Jenkins drags Mira to her feet and shoves her toward the door.

"I think I'll start with her," he says over his shoulder. "Since you care for her so much."

"Please! Don't!" Eve pleads, and he stops in his tracks.

He turns and stalks over to the counter, returning with another syringe. Eve's heart pounds, her sluggish mind struggling to think of some way out. As Jenkins injects her again, icy numbness spreads through her veins. Her vision blurs, darkness creeping in at the edges. Just before she loses consciousness, Eve fixes her gaze on Mira's terrified face.

I'm sorry, she thinks. *I tried...*

27

Scott drags his feet up his front steps after another eighteen-hour day of fruitless searching for Eve. He collapses onto the faded couch, too exhausted even to remove his muddy boots or hat.

It has been three weeks since he begged the media for answers, and they'd moved on to better ratings, abandoning his missing wife to yesterday's news. Reed and Morris no longer meet his hollow-eyed stare, mouths pressed into pitiful lines—there are only so many fruitless double shifts you can pull on a dead-end case.

But Scott will never stop scanning crowds, questioning locals, and searching abandoned barns like the other weepy family members in the support group that was suggested. Despite everyone else writing Eve off as long gone, his gut screams she is hidden close—so close he can almost smell her shampoo on the wind most nights. Most folks call that wishful thinking or obsession. Scott calls it hope.

In the kitchen, a clatter breaks the house's thick silence. Scott bolts upright, waiting to hear Eve's lilting "Sorry! I'm such a klutz..."

But there is nothing, save the hum of the empty fridge.

His gut lurches, air crushed from him in a ragged gasp. Habit and memory betray him every moment she isn't here, the house sheltering the ghost of a vibrant woman the town wrote off as dead weeks ago. He curses his foolish belief Eve might return as if from some errand like everyone whispers behind their pitying eyes.

But a blunt smack upside the head by gritty reality won't absolve him from chasing vapor and shadows until Eve is safe at home or he is with her on the other side. He hardly remembers what life was like before her—and he doesn't want to. Even breathing without Eve is an unbearable burden. So Scott will pick himself up tomorrow just before dawn, suit up for the long day ahead, and continue shouldering the weight...no matter the cost. What choice does he have?

28

The old farmhouse looms before Eve, its worn wooden siding and chipping paint concealing untold terrors within.

Jenkins marches them up creaking steps to a pair of oak doors, shoving them open with a crash.

"Welcome to your new home, ladies." His smile is all teeth, jagged and yellow. "Things are going to be different around here from now on. We're gonna be family. I'm gonna ease up on your medicines some...and tomorrow...tomorrow we garden."

Eve's stomach churns at the thought of being trapped in the main house with him and his make-believe wife. She recalls what Mira told her when she first arrived, that they'd be shuffled between structures on the property. Eve exchanges a wary glance with Mira, whose eyes are dull and hollow with defeat.

Jenkins gestures grandly around the living area, to the chairs where he binds Eve and then Mira. Once he's finished, he looks around, a smug smile on his face. "Spacious, no? And the gardens —you'll love tending to my prize roses. I do so value beauty and order."

His predatory gaze lingers on Eve. She suppresses a shudder, her spine straightening and her chin lifting in defiance. She will not cower before this monster.

When Jenkins leaves to "prepare their room," Eve seizes the opportunity.

"We can't stay here," she hisses to Mira. "He's completely unhinged."

Mira's lips tighten. "You don't know the half of it. The others..." She swallows hard. "Once he moves them to the main house—none of them made it out alive."

Eve's blood runs cold. So her suspicions were correct. She grips Mira's arm, a spark of determination igniting within.

"Then we'll be the first. We have to get out of here, and soon, before it's too late."

Mira searches her face, and for the first time Eve spies a flicker of life in her pale eyes. She nods once, jaw set with grim purpose.

Before Eve can manage a response or formulate a concrete plan, Jenkins returns and drags them, stumbling, into the modest dining room, gesturing for them to sit. The table is already set with worn china, as if for a dinner party.

Eve and Mira exchange another wary look, taking their seats. Jenkins sits at the head of the table, smiling benevolently at them.

"Tonight, we shall have a proper welcome dinner. I've prepared all your favorites." He snaps his fingers, and a young boy in a white jacket emerges from the kitchen, carrying a tray of unrecognizable meat and raw onions.

Eve frowns, confused by the boy's presence. He can't be more than ten years old, eyes sunken and skin pale. The pungent, metallic scent turns Eve's stomach. She eyes the lumps of "meat" warily as the boy deposits some onto her plate. She notices bruises circling his wrist. Eve feels bile rise into her throat as the pieces click into place.

Jenkins waves a hand, dismissing the boy. "He's a recent acquisition. So much potential, if only he had proper guidance." His gaze darkens. "But some lessons must be learned the hard way."

He nods to Eve. "Eat, or you'll see what I mean."

Eve forces herself to take a bite of her meal, unable to tamper her gag reflex. She avoids Mira's gaze, afraid of what she might see in the other woman's eyes. They are trapped in a house of horrors, at the mercy of a psychopath, and now, seeing the boy, she knows it is far worse than she thought. The only silver lining, if Eve could even call it that—is that with a missing child, more people would be searching.

Jenkins chatters on about his prize roses and other mundane topics, as if this were any normal dinner. But his true madness slips through in flashes—a deranged glint in his pale eyes, a peculiar cadence to his speech.

Eve pushes the unidentified meat around her plate, nausea threatening to overwhelm her.

She waits until Jenkins leaves the room, citing some chore he must attend to in the kitchen. As soon as he disappears from view, she turns to Mira with quiet urgency.

"We have to go. Now, tonight, *before*—" She swallows hard. "Before he kills one of us. We have to get that kid out of here."

Mira nods, her face pale but resolute. "I know. But how? He has the woods booby-trapped, and—"

"There has to be something here we can use as a weapon..." Eve's mind races as she considers their options. None are ideal, but there is no other choice. They will die if they don't find a way out. She senses the tides changing in Jenkins's moods.

"The doors and windows are all locked or boarded up," Mira says. "He planned this very carefully. We would have to physically overpower him, and he's twice our size."

Eve shakes her head, refusing to accept defeat. "There has to be something. We can't just sit here and wait to become his next victims, and we can't let him keep hurting that kid..."

Her gaze lands on the antique vase in the center of the table.

"It's risky," Mira warns. "I don't know..." She glances toward the back door, worry etched into her features.

Eve pushes back her chair and gets to her feet, waddling on the restraints. "I want to check something."

She creeps toward the back door, ears straining for any sign of Jenkins's approach. The house is eerily silent around her, as if holding its breath in anticipation of the events about to unfold.

Heart pounding, she crosses to the back door, just off the dining room. The thick wooden door looks warped and weathered, but intact. She grips the handle and twists, though she already knows what she'll find.

Locked.

The deadbolt is solid iron, far older than any modern lock. Eve rattles the handle in frustration, then runs her hands along the door's edges, frame and hinges. No hidden latches or easy way to break through. Jenkins was telling the truth—all exits have been sealed shut.

With a frustrated sigh, Eve steps back and surveys the room, seeking anything they might use to aid their escape. The vase on the table catches her eye again, smooth porcelain gleaming dully in the low light. It looks heavy, but unwieldy. Still, a weapon is a weapon when lives are at stake.

Eve peers through the window in the door. The overgrown garden is dimly lit by the moon overhead, shadows clinging to every tree and bush. Somewhere in that tangle of darkness lay the remains of Jenkins's victims, their bones mingling with the roots of roses and tulips.

She swallows hard against the bile rising in her throat and turns to Mira. A floorboard groans behind her. Eve whirls around as Jenkins emerges from the shadows of the kitchen. His eyes gleam with madness, lips curled into a sinister sneer.

"Going somewhere, ladies?" He takes a step forward, all predatory grace and coiled strength. "I'm afraid it's past your bedtime."

29

Alone in her dingy motel room, Lucy let the half-empty bottle of wine slip from her lifeless fingertips. The smell of alcohol filled the air as she sunk deeper into a drunken haze, memories rising up to taunt her.

"Are you kidding me?" She slammed her hand against the steering wheel in frustration as their rental car sputtered and died on a desolate stretch of coastal highway. The setting sun cast an orange glow over the ocean's surface, but Lucy couldn't appreciate its beauty in her current state.

Eve glanced out at the sunset before placing a comforting hand on Lucy's arm. "We'll be fine, Luce. Probably just needs a jump. I'll call AAA."

But after thirty minutes on hold with no success, they were told that there was nothing they could do until morning. Frustration and anger boiled inside of Lucy as she kicked the tire in her strappy heels. "Now what?"

Suddenly, an old pickup truck rattled toward them. Heat stirred inside Lucy as she eyed the driver—muscular and tanned, with kind eyes. Precisely the kind of trouble she was looking for.

"Evening, ladies." He tipped his cowboy hat. "Scott Collins. Need some help?"

As Scott popped the hood, Lucy leaned seductively over the car, giving him an ample view down her low-cut blouse. But to her surprise, Scott seemed unfazed by her charms. His gaze was fixed on Eve, a bashful smile forming on his lips.

It turned out that Scott was just passing through town and staying at a fishing lodge up the beach. He even gave Eve his number in case they needed help again. As they drove off with Scott's number and a functioning car, Lucy seethed with envy. So this handsome stranger got to play hero while golden girl Eve got her own little fairytale?

"This trip was supposed to be about me getting over Brad," Lucy fumed, shooting a harsh look at her sister. "And here you are flirting with some wannabe cowboy."

Eve blushed as Lucy continued her rant. "And don't forget, you're supposed to be getting engaged to Victor as soon as we get back. I already told Mom and Dad the good news, that their perfect daughter will finally make them happy by marrying the wealthy bachelor they've been pushing on you for years. So don't go off sneaking around with that redneck."

Eve opened her mouth to argue, but Lucy cut her off.

"We have a dinner planned with Victor's family as soon as we get back to celebrate your engagement. And I made sure it's somewhere classy, where dusty boots and cowboy hats aren't allowed. So get this silly fling out of your system now. Don't ruin your perfectly planned future over some weird fantasy. He will not be your white knight, Evie. From the looks of it, he doesn't have two pennies to rub together..."

Eve crossed her arms and turned away, staring out the window in silence. But over the next week, Lucy couldn't help but notice her sister slipping away for long "walks" whenever she could. And when she returned, Eve had a bright smile on her face, like Lucy's warning meant nothing.

By the end of their doomed vacation, not only was Eve single again, but she had also broken off her engagement with Victor over the phone.

And as they prepared to depart that seaside town for good, Lucy realized this was merely the latest fracture in their already strained relationship.

Over the years, golden girl Eve had unintentionally eclipsed Lucy too many times, stealing attention and accolades without even trying. And now she had tossed aside the perfect future that Lucy herself could only dream of, all for a whirlwind fling with a stranger.

Lucy swallowed back the familiar bitterness and envy. Maybe Eve was fearless in chasing her heart's desires, no matter the chaos left in her wake. Or maybe she was just selfish, never considering who she hurt along the way.

Either way, as the highway stretched on ahead of them into an uncertain future, Lucy vowed this would be the last time Eve's impulsive actions ruined her life. She was done living in her sister's shadow. From then on, Lucy promised herself one thing—whatever it took, she would never let Eve outshine her again.

30

Eve sags against the cabin wall, adrenaline crashing after her latest failed escape attempt. No matter how she scratched at door hinges or pried at floorboards, she can't get free. Jenkins is punishing her again, and exhaustion blankets her, but she fights against the urge to sleep. In lucid moments, Eve clings to memories of better days to maintain sanity—picnic dates with Scott along the river, girls' nights with Lucy laughing over wine.

But bleaker thoughts creep in, too. What if she never again tastes fresh air or sees sunlight? Or Scott's smile fades from her memory until he becomes a shadow? Her sister marrying without Eve to stand at her side?

She glances upward, as if she can will herself through the locked door. What deranged purpose did Jenkins have keeping her here? Ransom? Revenge? Or just a sadist's twisted pleasure?

Eve shudders, her imagination conjuring darker fates than she cares to dwell on. This helplessness terrifies her. But she pushes down the panic, steadying her breathing, just like her therapist taught her. She has to believe if she keeps a clear head, an opportunity will come.

Eve runs her thumb over her wedding band, drawing courage

from the engraved promise she and Scott had exchanged on their joyful, sunlit wedding day: "You and me, forever."

She's been here for months, but she can't lose hope. Her family needs her. Scott needs her. She will find a way back to them.

Eve hears Jenkins approach and begins scrubbing the floors, humming softly. That tune, the one he loathes. She asks about Mira and the boy. Jenkins ignores her. She keeps asking anyway.

Her heart races. This is a dangerous game, but she craves the thrill of defiance after so many days of being alone and numbed into submission.

Jenkins plops down in his armchair, pale eyes glinting. His knobby fingers clench around the worn armrests. "Stop that caterwauling. I told you to shut up."

Eve pauses, rag in hand, meeting his gaze. A surge of grim satisfaction rises in her chest at the sight of Jenkins trembling with barely contained rage. She knows this can go one of two ways, and she has to try both. She opens her mouth again, closes it, and starts to hum.

Jenkins lunges from his seat, gnarled hands outstretched. Eve scrambles back against the wall, a wild grin stretching her cracked lips.

He seizes her by the throat, cutting off her airway. Spots dance across her vision as she struggles against his iron grip.

"You foolish girl," he hisses. "I should have ended your miserable life long ago."

Eve rasps out a laugh, clutching at his hands. "Now is as good a time as any. Come on...it's what Edna wants, isn't it?"

Jenkins squeezes tighter, eyes bulging behind wire-rimmed spectacles. She can feel her windpipe collapsing, can taste blood on her tongue—

Then he releases her. Eve collapses to the floor, gasping and coughing, a mad laugh escaping her lips.

Jenkins stares down at her, chest heaving. There is something unhinged in his pale gaze now, a shattered fragility beneath the rage.

Eve drags herself upright, wiping blood from her mouth. Her throat burns, but triumph flickers inside her. She has found his weakness.

Jenkins backs away, hands trembling. For the first time, Eve sees real fear in his eyes.

"You're going to pay for that," he rasps. But his usual vitriol has deserted him, and he walks out of the room.

In the reflection of a metal pot, Eve examines the split in her lip, wincing at the sting. But beneath the pain is a surge of pride. She's found the crack in Jenkins's armor at last.

When he walks back into the room, she is waiting with a mocking grin, blood staining her teeth. Jenkins averts his gaze, pale eyes darting about in distress.

"What's the matter?" Eve asks softly. "Can't stomach the sight of your handiwork?"

Jenkins ignores her, hastily gathering cleaning supplies. His hands shake so badly he can barely hold the mop.

Eve sidles closer, lowering her voice to a conspiratorial whisper. "I know your secret now. I know why you can never finish the job. You're weak, Jenkins. You always have been."

He whirls on her, eyes wild behind his spectacles. "Be silent!"

Eve laughs. "Or what? You'll choke me again?"

Jenkins hurls the mop at her feet, chest heaving. "Enough of your games!" he shrieks. "Do you think I won't punish you for your insolence?"

"You can certainly try." Eve folds her arms, utterly unconcerned. "But we both know you're afraid to get your hands dirty. You're pathetic, Jenkins. Edna would be ashamed of you."

Jenkins stares at her, mouth twisting. Then he turns on his heel and storms from the cabin, slamming the door so hard the walls shake.

Eve smiles, wiping blood from her chin. Her lip is split, and her throat is raw, but she has won this round.

Or so she thinks.

Later, Eve staggers as Jenkins shoves her into the torture shed, the rusted door groaning behind them. Shadows swarm at the edges of her vision, the blood pounding in her ears nearly drowning out Jenkins's taunts.

She grips the rotted wooden post, vision flickering, and forces herself to meet his pale gaze. "You're afraid," she rasps. "A pathetic coward. That's why you can't finish the job."

Jenkins's face contorts with rage, spittle flying from his lips. "Shut up! I'll give you something to cry about." He seizes a coil of barbed wire from the wall, the rusted metal scraping against wood.

Eve clenches her jaw, refusing to look away. "Go on then. Show me what you got."

The wire whip cracks like a gunshot, its barbs raking across the flesh of her back. Pain explodes through her skull, but she holds his gaze, rage burning in her chest like a star about to go supernova.

"The police know where I am," she hisses. "Edna told them, and they're coming for you. It's only a matter of time."

Jenkins blinks, a flicker of doubt passing over his features. His hands tighten around the whip, knuckles whitening until the coil begins to unwind and tumble to the floor, forgotten.

"Edna is dead."

Eve raises her brow. "Wrong. I am Edna."

His eyes glaze over, gaze turning inward. "Edna?" he whispers softly. "Is that really you?"

Eve watches, heart in her throat, as his grip on reality starts to slip. She sags against her restraints, pulse slowing to a steady pound of victory.

Checkmate.

31

The cabin creaks in the howling wind. Eve lies on her stomach on the edge of her mattress, watching Jenkins through lowered lashes. He slumps into his threadbare armchair, clutching a glass of whiskey.

Eve forces a tremor into her voice. "It must have been so hard without me."

Jenkins stiffens, and his knuckles pale around the glass. "What would you know about it? You left."

She shrugs, a delicate lift of one shoulder. "Losing the person you love most in the world...I can't imagine."

The slightest softening in his eyes. She presses on, angling her body toward him. "Remind me how we met…"

Jenkins swallows another gulp of whiskey. His gaze turns inward, drifting into the past. Eve slides closer, hands folded in her lap, the picture of quiet concern.

"We were high school sweethearts," he says hoarsely. "You know that, Edna. You were a cheerleader. I was quarterback of the football team. Everyone said we were meant to be."

Eve makes an encouraging noise, though bile rises in her

throat, and she has to choke back a hysterical laugh at the banality of it. Of course, Jenkins would pine for a cliché.

"We got married right out of school," Jenkins continues. "Had fifty blissful years together. Now you're gone, and..." His voice cracks. "I'm just so lonely."

Eve reaches out and grasps his hand. His fingers are cold and knobby in her grip. She summons tears to her eyes, blinking them onto her lashes.

"I know you love me very much," she whispers. "I know how special I am to you."

Jenkins looks up at her, eyes shining. "Do you? Is that why you came back?"

Eve squeezes his hand and offers a tremulous smile. "Of course. A love like ours is forever."

Jenkins stares at their joined hands, lost in memories of a love that probably never was.

Eve waits, heart pounding, wondering if the trap has finally snapped shut.

Jenkins clears his throat, pulling his hand from Eve's grasp. "Thank you for coming. It's been a comfort."

Eve ducks her head demurely. "You know I'll always find my way back to you."

When she glances up, Jenkins is watching her with an unreadable expression. She swallows hard—did she overplay her hand? But a moment later, his features soften into a smile.

"You're a good woman, Edna. I'm lucky you came into my life. I've always known that."

Eve's stomach churns at the comment, but she forces herself to return his smile. "As am I. You've given me so much, helping me see what's really important in life."

Jenkins stands, joints creaking. "I should let you get some rest. But I'll be thinking of you."

The threat behind his words makes Eve's skin crawl. She swallows hard and says, "And I, you."

Jenkins leaves, the door clanging shut behind him. Eve sags against the bed, pulse racing. Her gambit paid off—for now. She gained a glimpse into Jenkins's delusions, and he believes she's on his side.

But how long can she keep up the charade? And will it be enough to earn her freedom?

These questions plague Eve as she tosses and turns, getting little sleep. So she is surprised when Jenkins returns the next day earlier than usual. As he sets down her tray of food, he lingers instead of leaving right away. "I know you're not really her," he snaps. "I'm not crazy or confused. I know Edna is gone."

Eve blinks, caught off-guard by his forthrightness. She fumbles for a response. "I know you do. I didn't mean to imply otherwise."

Jenkins searches her face, as if gauging her sincerity. "Still, talking about her, about us, it brought me comfort. Made me feel less alone." His eyes plead for understanding. "Our conversation meant a great deal to me."

Eve forces a sympathetic smile. "I'm glad I could provide some solace. It's been so long since I've had someone to truly confide in."

She infuses her voice with enough wistful loneliness that Jenkins nods, features softening. He sits on the edge of her bed, close enough for Eve to smell his perpetually sour body odor.

"I want you to know, you can tell me anything," he says. His sudden intensity puts Eve on alert, even as he continues. "I'm here for you, to listen and provide counsel."

Eve swallows back bile and places a hand on his. His skin is cold and clammy. "Thank you. That means a lot."

He pats her hand, gaze turning shrewd. "You're not just saying that to humor me?"

She summons the tears that are never very far away, letting them spill onto her cheeks. "No, of course not. I would never lie to you."

Jenkins relaxes, appeased. "Good. Honesty and trust are so

important." His fingers curl around hers, a parody of affection. "You really are special, you know. So much like my Edna. I'm so happy your memory treatments are finally working..."

"It's been months. And you've been so diligent. Of course they're working."

"Good. That's good. I'm happy to hear it."

"How are Mira and Charlie?"

Jenkins looks perplexed. "Who's Charlie... and who's Mira?"

"The other people that live here."

He seems to contemplate it for a long time. "Oh, them. I call them something else."

"And how are they? I haven't seen them..."

He grins from ear to ear. "They're well and alive, my pet. That's all you need to know."

"Are you treating them as well as you're treating me? Edna would want that, you know."

Jenkins nods profusely. "Yes. Yes. Of course. Believe me, I know my Edna."

"You're not punishing them like you are me, right?"

He looks at Eve as though he's been sucker punched. "I thought you liked it here? I thought you were happy?"

"I am happy."

He looks relieved for a moment and then he chuckles nervously. "It's because you're so much like my Edna. I just never know what to expect from you, princess."

Eve forces herself not to recoil. She has him now, reeling him in like a fish on a line. All she has to do is keep jerking that line to keep him on the hook.

"Tell me more about Edna," she says softly. "I want to know everything."

Jenkins's eyes mist over. His grip on her hand turns painful, but she doesn't dare pull away. "She was my whole world," he says, voice ragged with remembered grief. "My sun, my stars, the beat of my heart."

Eve makes a sound of sympathy, hoping the anguish in her eyes reads as compassion instead of disgust. "You must have cherished every moment with her."

"Every moment," Jenkins echoes. He launches into a lengthy, rambling tale of his life with Edna. Eve listens with half an ear, watching him for any useful details or vulnerabilities to exploit.

His guard is down now, suspicion mollified by her performance. But Eve knows it's only a matter of time before he starts to doubt her again.

She'll enjoy this victory, fleeting as it is. But she must always, *always,* remain one step ahead.

Eve lets Jenkins ramble on, feigning interest while plotting her next move. He thinks he has her fooled, lulled into compliance. But Eve still has a card left to play.

32

Eve swallows the irritation rising in her throat as she lugs the old bucket from room to room, stopping to scrub and scour every dusty corner of the cabin. The coarse, bristled brush irritates her palms as she works, but she dares not slow down. As long as she focuses on each smudge of grime and sweep of her arm, she can ignore Jenkins's lingering presence as he writes at his desk nearby, pen scratching away.

Kneeling to swipe away dust low along the walls, Eve catches sight of a stack of flyers. Her heartbeat stills for just a moment before she hastily resumes her relentless scouring, hoping Jenkins hasn't noticed her pause over the papers. But truthfully, nothing escapes her captor's notice.

Eve can sense his pale eyes boring into her back even as she shifts to the next wall, stretching her tired limbs to reach the very top corners. Her shoulders burn but it is nothing compared to the slow fire kindling inside, waiting for a chance to investigate those strange flyers. She had only glimpsed them for a moment, but something about those papers looked almost familiar. Almost like—

"Getting all the nooks and crannies, I hope, my pet?" Jenkin's voice shatters her thoughts like a stone through glass. Eve flushes but doesn't turn around, not yet willing to let him scrutinize her face.

"Yes sir," Eve murmurs, dipping her brush with trembling hands. The lowered drug doses leave her system screaming, her whole body quaking uncontrollably. But she focuses on scrubbing, plotting her next move. Whatever dark secrets this house holds, she will uncover them. And somehow, turn them against the monster keeping her trapped here.

Giving up on a stubborn stain, Eve reaches for the stack of papers, but a sheet slips through her shaking grasp, fluttering to the floor like a wounded bird. Heart pounding, she grabs it and freezes. Her eyes scan the text—a plan detailing the forced erasure of her memory. Drugs, dosages, and other strange methods that make zero sense.

Eve struggles to calm her withdrawal-fueled trembling as Jenkins stands and crosses the room, demanding answers with predatory satisfaction.

“Aren’t you happy?” Jenkins says, eyeing the documents. “You don’t look happy.”

“I don’t understand…”

“What’s there to understand? Your treatment is complete.”

Her heart hammers in her chest, each beat echoing the betrayal that swells within her. She reads further, bile rising in her throat as she realizes the implications.

“Interesting read, no?” His voice slices through the tense silence, chilling her to the bone. Jenkins stands in the doorway, his expression gleaming with a sinister satisfaction.

"What is this?" Eve demands, thrusting the document toward him.

"Ah," he says, feigning surprise. "I see you've discovered our little arrangement."

"Arrangement?" She spits the word like venom.

"Indeed," Jenkins continues, unfazed. "You may not remember, but we met online, in a rather...unconventional forum."

Eve's mind races, grasping at fragments of memory. An ad on a bulletin board in town, and then a late-night chat room, an invitation to embrace the darkness within her. The thrill that coursed through her veins as she typed out her deepest desires.

"Your need for intensity was...palpable," Jenkins muses. "Our organization recognized your potential immediately. We offered you an escape from your mundane life, and you accepted."

"Accepted?" Eve's voice wavers, shock and anger warring within her. "You abducted me!"

"By your own request," Jenkins counters, smirking. "But, admittedly, we adjusted the terms of our agreement."

"Adjusted? You're a psychopath!" Eve shouts, rage boiling over.

"Perhaps," Jenkins concedes, his tone icy. "But you wanted this, my dear. You sought us out, craving danger and transformation. And now, here we are."

A sickening realization dawns on Eve. The bedroom walls close in around her as the truth sinks its teeth into her soul.

"This doesn't make sense ..." Eve whispers, her voice trembling. "When I agreed to be taken, I never thought you would drug me, hurt me, violate me, and try to kill me."

Jenkins smirks, his eyes glinting with a sinister light. "That reminds me of a story. Do you know the one about the frog and the scorpion?"

Eve's brow furrows, her mind racing to recall the fable.

"The frog let the scorpion ride on its back to the other side of the pond," Jenkins continues, his voice dripping with malice. "Along the way the scorpion stung the frog. Before she died, the frog asked, 'Why did you do that? I helped you.' And the scorpion replied, 'It's my nature, dear. I'm the scorpion Eve. That's what we do."

A chill runs down Eve's spine as the realization sinks in. She had trusted Jenkins, believed his promises of excitement and escape, but in the end, he had betrayed her in the most heinous way possible.

"You're a monster," she breathes, her eyes filling with tears.

"You knew what you were getting into Princess. You sought out the scorpion, and now you must face the consequences."

A single tear splashes onto the wooden floor, as if marking the moment of Eve's unraveling. She presses her palms against her temples, willing the memories to come flooding back. The room seems to spin, and she closes her eyes.

"Remember," Jenkins had said, his voice a twisted echo in her mind.

The world around her dissolves, replaced by the sterile glow of her laptop screen.

It was late, too late for anything good to come from scrolling through endless online forums. But there it was: the link, nestled among the anonymous avatars and cryptic usernames.

"Destiny awaits," read the caption beneath it. Intrigued, she clicked the link, expecting little more than a cheap thrill.

"Welcome," began the message that appeared, "to the Radical Escape Network."

"Are you tired of living your mundane life?" the chatbot asked, its tone dripping with the pretense of concern. "Are you ready to shake things up?"

"Is this...real?" Eve typed out.

"Only as real as you want it to be," came the reply.

"Then yes," she wrote, surprising even herself. "I want something different. I want to feel alive again."

"Excellent," was the response. "We'll be in touch."

Her present reality comes crashing back, and Eve is met with the grim irony of her situation. She had sought to escape one precarious situation, only to find herself locked within another, darker one.

"See?" Jenkins's voice slices through the silence, his words laced with sardonic wit. "You chose this path, remember?"

"Never like this," she whispers, fists clenched at her sides. "This wasn't the plan."

"Plans change," he counters, shrugging nonchalantly. "You wanted excitement, a break from the ordinary. And now, you have it."

"Excitement? " Eve snarls, her voice rising in pitch. "You call this excitement?"

"Call it what you will," Jenkins smirks, leaning against the doorframe with a self-satisfied air. "But remember, you were the one who reached out to us. You were the one seeking danger."

"Enough!" she cries, choking on her own fury and despair. "I never asked for this nightmare. I only wanted—"

"Ah, but isn't that always the way?" he muses, his grin widening. "People are never satisfied with what they have. They crave the unknown, the dangerous, the forbidden. And then, when they find themselves immersed in it, they cry out for the safety of their former lives."

Eve's breath comes in ragged gasps, her vision blurred by tears. She knows the truth in his words, and the realization cuts deeper than any knife ever could.

She sits on the shabby, stained mattress that tops Jenkins bed, her eyes darting from the chains that bind her ankles to Jenkins, his gaunt face a portrait of twisted delight.

"Listen," she says, trying to keep her voice steady, "I only wanted this as a means to an end. I thought...I thought it would help me access my trust fund."

"Ah, yes," Jenkins drawls, feigning sympathy. "Your precious inheritance. The golden ticket out of that tedious existence you got yourself trapped in. And you thought we'd be your partners in crime?"

"Something like that," she admits, hating herself for the desperation that seeps into her words. "But the plan was never for you to keep me here indefinitely. You were supposed to contact my family for ransom, and then release me."

"True," he concedes, his lips curling into a cruel smile. "But plans change—and sometimes for the better."

"Better?" she scoffs, anger surging within her. "You call this better? "

"Indeed," he replies, still placid despite her outburst. "You see, I've taken quite a liking to you, my dear. Your resourcefulness...your wit...your stubborn defiance. It's all so very...entertaining."

"Entertaining? You've kept me so drugged up I can't even remember my own name half the time." As the words leave her mouth, Eve's heart hammers against her ribcage. "You're sick, you know that?"

"Perhaps," he allows, the corners of his eyes crinkling with amusement. "But it doesn't change the fact that you're mine now. And I have no intention of letting you go."

"Please," she pleads, the weight of her situation pressing down on her chest like a thousand-pound boulder. "I won't say anything to anyone, I swear. Just let me go, and I'll disappear. You'll never see me again. And you can keep the money…"

"Ah, but that's where you're wrong," he says. The shadows in the room deepen as his voice drops to a menacing whisper and he comes closer. "I want to see you, Eve. I want to watch you struggle and squirm, like a trapped fly in my web. It's exhilarating, don't you think?"

"Please," she gasps, her heart leaping into her throat. "You don't have to do this."

"Of course not," he agrees, leaning in close, so close she can feel the intensity of his gaze on her. "But I want to."

Eve's mind races, searching for any shred of hope, any chance of escape from this hellish nightmare. But as the darkness closes in around her, she knows, with chilling certainty, that the only way out is through the twisted labyrinth of Jenkins's demented games. And she has no choice but to play along.

33

Eve scrubs her body with renewed vigor, the pungent scent of lye soap filling the drafty shed. A spark lights her eyes for the first time in weeks. Tonight, everything changes.

As she peeks through the worn boards, Eve's gaze darts about, identifying each component she and Mira secretly gathered and hid in the vent behind a loose slat they pried free. It's not much—a rusted hammer, a broken fork, some moth-eaten socks—but these paltry items will have to do, scavenged and smuggled one by one whenever Jenkins turned his back.

It took endless patience and care, but the two women compiled what they needed for their haphazardly plotted bid for escape. Tonight, during Jenkins's weekly supply run into town, they would finally break free of this waking nightmare.

Eve's heart pounds with equal parts nervous excitement and dread. She thinks of the revolver and the hunting knife Jenkins keeps strapped to his waist at all times. And the countless traps he has set. But she steels her resolve. The alternative—remaining helpless captives until Jenkins decides to dispose of them—is unthinkable.

When Jenkins returns Eve from the shed to the house, she

looks for the boy. Jenkins has been keeping him locked in the cabin, but Eve suspects he has been brought to the house for Jenkins's vile amusement. She intends to find where.

A creak sounds from the hallway. Eve's heart seizes—but it's only Mira, carrying fresh linens for their normal housekeeping routine. Up close, Eve sees new worry lines etching Mira's face. They exchange a subtle glance charged with anticipation. Only a few more hours remain until they implement their desperate plan.

As soon as Jenkins leaves on his supply errand, they'll spring into action. Locate the boy, gather their makeshift supplies, and disappear into the woods before Jenkins returns. Every time Eve considers how exposed and vulnerable they'll be outside in those woods, her throat constricts in panic. But it's too late for second thoughts now.

She clings to the hope that soon her manipulations of Jenkins won't matter. Once she and Mira get free, they can disappear into new lives where men like him will never find them again.

In the evenings, Eve and Mira whisper final details, accounting for anything that could go awry once Jenkins leaves. Mira frets over the possibility of unseen alarms or traps. She worries this is just another of Jenkins's head games, giving them hope before quashing it cruelly. Eve nods along, her jaw set and her eyes gleaming with a fierce determination.

As Mira wrings her hands, Eve grips her fingers and says point-blank, "We have to bring the kid when we run—abandoning a child to Jenkins's appetites is unthinkable."

Mira bites her lip, conflict etched across her pallid face. "Eve, please see reason. He's little, and he has no stamina. He's dead weight that could kill our only chance..."

Eve gives one firm shake of her head, jaw set. "Yes, but we can't leave him to that monster." She shudders, remembering the boy's sunken eyes, his bruises.

Mira squeezes her eyes shut against welling tears. Softening her tone, Eve continues, "I understand the tremendous risk going back for him poses, and what it will mean to bring him along. But we can't abandon him, Mira. We just can't."

Silent resignation wars with dawning purpose on Mira's face. Finally, she dips her chin in terse agreement, mouth thinning into an apprehensive line. "I guess we'll have to take turns carrying him. God help us."

"It's a bad idea," Mira adds.

"I know." Eve nods. "But sometimes bad ideas refuse to go away."

"I just hope you know what you're doing."

Eve shrugs. She remembers the way the boy curled into her that first night after she saw him at dinner, seeking rare kindness in this cruel place. "It isn't a choice."

"I was a teacher," Mira says. "And I know kids. *Everything* is a choice. We can come back for him."

"We may not make it back."

Tears prick Mira's eyes. "Exactly."

As the sun sets, orange and hazy, tension thrums in Eve's veins, threatening to choke her. So much now relies on flawless execution of their risky plan. Jenkins will only be gone a few hours at most. Fleeing into the wilderness with a child in tow seems impossible. She imagines a hundred different ways it could all go horribly wrong. But the alternative—passively awaiting whatever fate Jenkins intends for them—is the only truly unthinkable option.

Whatever happens tonight, Eve vows, they will taste freedom again. Or die trying.

She almost doesn't hear Jenkins calling her name, startling her from her reverie. The time has come. Eve sucks in a deep breath and turns to face him, chin held high.

34

Lucy raps her knuckles on the faded hotel room door. It swings open to reveal the disheveled private investigator her parents hired. Without waiting for an invitation, she brushes past him into the dim room. Her heeled boots click sharply across the worn floors as she makes a beeline for the desk.

"Please, have a seat," the detective says, nodding at the chair.

Lucy ignores him. "It's been weeks. What progress have you made in finding my sister?"

The detective sinks onto the bed with a weary sigh. "Miss Burke, as I've explained, these cases take time—"

"That's not good enough," Lucy cuts in. She plants her palms on his desk and leans in. "My family is paying you a fortune to find Eve. So where is she?"

The detective rubs his temples. "I understand your frustration. But we're working every lead. The problem is we're starting from very little information. Your sister's laptop is still being processed, and it's been difficult getting access to her phone records and search history."

Lucy's eyes flash. "I don't care about your excuses. My parents are very influential people. If you can't get the information you need, then you're useless."

The detective's jaw tightens, but he keeps his voice level. "With all due respect, even money and connections can only do so much. Investigations take time, especially without much evidence to go on."

"That's bullshit," Lucy snaps. "Eve is out there, scared or hurt, while you sit around pushing papers. What are you even doing to find her?"

The detective meets her glare. "I understand this is a difficult situation, but getting upset with me won't help. I promise we're utilizing every resource to locate your sister."

Lucy straightens up and smooths out her shirt, composing herself. "Forget it. Clearly, coming here was a mistake. This was a dead end—*you're* just another dead end. I'll find her myself."

She turns on her heel, letting the door slam behind her. Alone in the hall, Lucy can't help but feel a tiny flicker of satisfaction at putting that incompetent waste in his place. She meant what she said—one way or another, she'll be the one to find Eve. Which is exactly how it should be.

35

Eve's pulse thrums as Jenkins's eyes narrow, his gaze combing the room. She forces her fists to uncurl, plastering a guileless smile across her face.

"Darling," she calls out, injecting false cheer into her voice, "You called?"

"What are y'all yapping about in there?"

"Yapping?" Eve shrugs. "We're just doing our chores."

"What chores?"

"Finished folding the linens," she chirps. "Did you need any help with dinner?"

Jenkins grunts, rubbing his temples. "Feeling under the weather. Don't think I'll head into town today."

Eve's stomach sinks. This wasn't part of the plan. She takes a slow breath, mind racing.

"Oh no, I'm sorry to hear that," she says lightly. "I know how you look forward to your evening cards with the boys. Say, I could fix you up some of Edna's remedy—that always perks you right up."

Jenkins's face softens at the mention of his late wife. "No, no, just feeling my age today. I suppose I could stop in for a quick drink..."

"Here," Eve says. "While you get ready, why don't you tell me more about Edna?"

Jenkins looks at her, dumbfounded. "You already know about my Edna..."

"Yes, love. But there's always more to know about a woman..."

He nods. "I suppose you're right."

"What was she like?"

His pale blue eyes narrow, but he takes the bait, his obsession with his dead spouse too all-consuming to resist. "She was...perfect," he murmurs, momentarily entranced by the memory.

"Really?" Eve presses, her mind racing as she considers the plan she and Mira have devised. "How so?"

"Her hair, it was so soft," he reminisces.

"Sounds lovely," Eve replies, her voice trembling despite her best efforts. She ignores the dread pooling in her gut, focusing on the memory of Scott's face—his rugged features, steadfast loyalty, and love that had endured even her darkest betrayals.

"Her voice was like a songbird..." Jenkins continues, lost in his delusion.

Eve nods, her eyes darting between Jenkins and Mira. Every second feels like a lifetime, a reminder that their window of opportunity is rapidly closing. The gravity of their situation threatens to engulf her, but she clings to her resourcefulness and wit like a lifeline.

"Her eyes," Jenkins says, his voice catching. "The way they looked at me...I've never felt so loved."

"Until now?" Eve quips, her sardonic smile masking the terror gnawing at her insides. She watches as Jenkins's expression shifts from wistful to dangerous, and she knows they're out of time.

"Indeed," he hisses, suspicion sparking in his gaze once more. "Until now."

Eve's heart skips a beat, and she shares a tense glance with

Mira. Their plan hangs by a thread, balanced on the edge of triumph and disaster, and Eve can't help but crave the dangerous thrill of it all.

"Jenkins," she says, forcing a laugh, "you're such an enigma."

"Am I?" he replies, his eyes boring into hers as if searching for any hidden secrets.

"Absolutely," she insists, putting all her persuasive prowess into keeping him at bay. "You're a mystery wrapped in a riddle inside an enigma."

"Interesting choice of words," he murmurs, the ghost of a smile playing on his lips.

"Is it?" she counters, praying that their luck holds just a little longer, and he decides drinking away from home is the best plan of action after all.

The cabin walls close in around Eve. Sweat beads on her brow as Jenkins forces her and Mira to their bedroom and secures their binds.

He eyes her with suspicion as he lifts the bottle from the nightstand. "You're too quiet tonight. What's going on in that scheming little head of yours?"

Her pulse thunders. *Stay calm. Think fast.*

"I just can't stop thinking of Edna. You never talk about her anymore."

Jenkins stiffens. His knuckles pale around the glass. "Why do you keep talking about Edna?"

"I just want to make sure I'm living up to your expectations."

The old man stares into the amber liquid, lost in memory. His eyes mist over. "You could never."

Eve silently prays. *Come on, you pathetic fool. Take the bait.* She secretly hopes he'll leave and be pulled over as he's already inebriated. Regardless, she needs him gone.

"She was an angel," he rasps. "So beautiful. We were soulmates."

"It must hurt so much to lose your soulmate." She infuses her voice with empathy. "No wonder you still miss her."

Jenkins exhales a shuddering sigh. Right on cue, he stands and heads for the door. "I need a drink. At the bar. Alone."

As soon as the door slams behind him, Eve bolts into action.

Her hands shake a little as she fumbles with her restraints. Mira watches her, wide-eyed and trembling, a mixture of fear and hope etched across her face. The seconds tick away like a metronome in Eve's mind, urging her to work faster.

Finally, with a thud that echoes through the room, the restraints fall away and Eve is free. She moves swiftly to Mira's side, undoing her binds with practiced precision. The relief that washes over them is palpable, but they know they can't let their guard down just yet.

Eve eyes the bedroom door, her mind racing with options. They can't risk encountering Jenkins again, not now that they're so close to escaping this hellish nightmare. They need to find the boy and get out of this house as quickly as possible.

Silently, Eve motions for Mira to follow her as they slip out of the bedroom and into the dimly lit hallway. Their footsteps are soft against the worn wooden floorboards, but each creak reverberates through the eerie silence of the cabin. They hold their breath, listening for any sign of Jenkins's return.

With trembling hands, Eve pushes open the nearest door, revealing what appears to be a study. Moonlight streams through the small window, casting long shadows on the walls adorned with shelves overflowing with books and trinkets. But there is no sign of the boy.

Disheartened but determined, they continue their search, checking each room one by one. The house feels like a labyrinth, its corridors winding and twisting, leading them deeper into its dark secrets. As they pass an old oak door covered in peeling paint, Mira's heart skips a beat.

"I have a feeling about this room," she whispers to Eve. "Something tells me he might be in there."

Eve nods, her eyes gleaming with a blend of hope and trepidation. They approach the door and exchange another glance, silently communicating the gravity of their next move. With a deep breath, Eve twists the doorknob, and it creaks open to reveal a room shrouded in darkness. The air inside is heavy, thick with the scent of decay and neglect. Their eyes strain to adjust to the dim light filtering through tattered curtains.

As they step cautiously into the room, the floorboards groan under their weight. A flicker of movement catches Eve's attention, and she freezes, her heart pounding in her chest. A pair of glowing eyes stares back at her from the corner of the room. It takes a moment for her mind to register what she's seeing.

36

Eve blinks against the darkness. There, huddled in the gloom, is the boy they've been searching for. His face is dirty and streaked with tears, his clothes torn and tattered. His small frame trembles with fear as he curls himself into a tight ball.

Her heart breaks at the sight. She kneels down slowly, keeping her voice gentle and soothing. "Hey," she whispers, extending a hand toward the trembling boy. "It's okay. We're here to help you."

The boy flinches back, his eyes wide with terror. He huddles even closer to the corner of the room, as if trying to disappear into the shadows. Eve exchanges a worried glance with Mira, both of them realizing the extent of the trauma this child must have endured.

"We won't hurt you," Mira says softly, her voice filled with empathy. "We want to get you out of here."

Eve inches closer, careful not to startle the boy any further. She can see the fear etched into every line of his face, the hopelessness in his eyes. How many times had he been subjected to Jenkins's sadistic games? How much pain had he endured in this house of horrors?

"I promise you," Eve whispers, her voice choked with emotion, "we won't let him hurt you anymore. We're going to get you out of here, to a safe place."

The boy's eyes flicker with a glimmer of trust, his small frame relaxing ever so slightly. It's that flicker of hope that fuels Eve's determination to protect him at all costs. She reaches out again, this time resting a hand on his trembling shoulder.

"Let us help you," she says, her voice filled with conviction. "You don't have to be afraid anymore."

As if the touch has broken through some invisible barrier, the boy finally uncurls himself from the corner of the room. His eyes search Eve's face for any signs of deception, but all he finds is unwavering resolve.

"What's your name?" Mira asks softly, stepping closer to join them.

The boy hesitates for a moment, his gaze dropping to the floor. Then, in a voice barely above a whisper, he replies, "Charlie."

Eve's heart swells with relief and renewed purpose. "It's nice to meet you, Charlie. My name is Eve, and this is my friend Mira." She extends a gentle hand. "Let's get you out of here, okay?"

Charlie nods, some of the fear receding from his eyes. He takes Eve's hand, and she helps him slowly to his feet.

Just then, a booming crash shatters the silence. Eve's blood turns to ice. Footsteps thunder down the hall, growing louder. Jenkins.

"He's back," Mira gasps.

Eve's mind races. She knows now he never left, not really. There's no time to flee, nowhere to hide. She pushes Charlie behind her and turns to face the door, primal instinct taking over.

The door explodes inward and Jenkins looms in the doorway, reeking of liquor. His face contorts with rage when he sees Eve and Mira free.

"You deceitful whores!" he roars. "Thought you could escape me?"

He lunges, but Eve is ready. She ducks under his wild swing

and drives her elbow into his stomach. Jenkins staggers back with a grunt.

Before Eve can press the attack, Jenkins pulls a gun from his waistband. "Don't move!"

Eve freezes, her eyes locked on the barrel aimed at her chest. Jenkins's hand trembles with drunken rage.

“On your knees!” When Eve hesitates, Jenkins turns the gun on Mira and Charlie. "Now!"

Slowly, Eve sinks to her knees, hands raised in surrender. Mira pulls Charlie close, shielding his eyes.

Jenkins marches over and wrenches Charlie away. He shoves the boy into a nearby closet and slams the door shut. Charlie's muffled cries echo from within.

With Charlie locked away, Jenkins grabs Eve and Mira, binding their wrists.

He shoves Mira into their shared bedroom and slams the door. Then he drags Eve down the hall, throwing her into his private room.

"Take off your clothes," he demands, his eyes wandering over her body.

Revulsion rises in Eve's throat, but she complies, desperate to buy time. Jenkins approaches, reeking of liquor, and forces her down onto the bed.

"You're mine now," he growls, his cold fingers gripping her. "I'm going to teach you a lesson you won't soon forget."

Eve meets his cruel eyes unflinchingly, her gaze steady and resolute, even as her pulse hammers beneath her skin. She won't give him the satisfaction of seeing her fear.

Jenkins' scarred lips twist into a sadistic grin. "When I'm through with you, you'll wish you never tried to defy me."

37

Jenkins lunges forward, his weight crushing Eve beneath him. She thrashes, trying to buck him off, but he's too heavy. He pins her wrists above her head, his fingers digging into her flesh. His breath is hot and sour against her cheek. She can feel his erection pressing against her thigh.

"Please," she whimpers. "Please, don't."

But Jenkins just laughs. "Oh, Eve," he says, his voice dripping with mock sympathy. "You should have known better than to try to escape. You're mine forever."

He forces himself inside her, tearing through her defenses with a brutal swiftness that leaves her broken and sobbing. She fights him, but it's no use. He's too strong. Too determined.

When he's finished, he rolls off her, leaving her struggling for air and writhing in pain. She can feel the dampness between her legs, a confused mix of blood and something warm and sticky.

"Clean yourself up," Jenkins commands, kicking her leg aside.

Eve looks down to see a small stream of blood trickling between her thighs. She wants to scream, to fight back, but the strength has drained from her body. Her mind is a whirl of confusion and despair.

She reaches for a towel, dabbing at the wound, trying to stanch the flow of blood.

Jenkins watches her, a cruel smile playing on his lips. "You know, Eve," he says, leaning closer to her, "you're not the first. And you won't be the last."

Eve's eyes widen, her heart pounding in her chest as she realizes the extent of his cruelty. She is not surprised, but to hear him say it so casually...

Jenkins sighs, running a hand through his greasy hair. "You see, Eve, I have a...hobby. A little game I like to play. It's really quite simple. I find a woman, someone vulnerable, someone lost. And then I take her, keep her, use her. It's not personal, you understand? It's just...fun. A way to pass the time. A little excitement in an otherwise mundane life."

Eve listens, her mind reeling. She wants to scream, to fight back, but the words stick in her throat. She can feel her mind slipping away, the things she's done, the things she's seen slipping into darkness.

Jenkins cackles, sensing her defeat. "Don't worry, Eve. You'll get used to it. You'll learn to enjoy it, even. The more you submit, the more I'll care for you."

As the night draws on, Jenkins becomes increasingly unhinged, his maniacal laughter echoing through the darkened walls. Eve curls up in a ball on the cold floor, feeling the dampness seeping into her bones as she trembles with fear.

When she asks about Mira and Charlie, Jenkins goes silent. Eve has always made sure to be the one who would have to endure his wrath. Partly, so she'd remain his “favorite,” and partly to spare the others.

She’s about to cry out again, hoping Mira will shout back or give her a sign that she and Charlie are okay, when suddenly, Jenkins marches into the room, a vase of roses in his hand.

He sets the vase on the nightstand and carefully places the

roses next to the bloodied towel that Eve used to clean herself. He leans in close.

"Now, princess, you have something pretty to remember our time together. And if you ever try to escape again, I'll bury you under the rosebush that gave us these flowers."

He laughs, a twisted and chilling sound that sends shivers down Eve's spine. She knows he's not joking.

38

Jenkins rattles Eve awake, bellowing something about escorting her to the shower, the daily ritual she dreads above all else. But this time, as soon as he unlocks her handcuffs, Eve grabs the vase from her bedside table and smashes it over Jenkins's head. He stumbles back with a groan, hand flying to his bleeding scalp. Eve doesn't hesitate—she shoves past his enormous frame and flees out the front door.

Frigid winter air shocks Eve's lungs as she bursts outside, alone and unbound for the first time in months. The forest extends endlessly in all directions, the skeletal trees foreboding, yet beckoning under the steely sky.

Gasping breaths create puffs of steam as Eve plunges into the woods with no direction but away. She must put distance between herself and the nightmare she's been living, as much as her agonized feet and still-injured ankle can manage.

As Eve crashes through the underbrush, she considers Mira and the boy still trapped in that house. For a split second, she wonders if she should turn back and save them, too? But the pain shooting up her legs swiftly dashes that hope. She can barely save herself right now. At least by drawing Jenkins away, she's giving them this one chance to break free themselves. It's up to Mira now. Eve prays she has the courage to take the boy and run.

The further Eve goes, the more her adrenaline fades, leaving searing pain in its wake. Her feet feel shredded inside the tattered socks, each gnarled root and jagged stone another spike of agony. The thin sleep clothes Jenkins provided barely mute the bite of winter's chill. Still, she pushes on through her suffering, Jenkins's enraged shouts at her back spurring her forward.

When Eve can no longer run, she slows her pace and staggers into unfamiliar terrain. Has she gone in circles? Eve stops all together, gasping. She strains for any hopeful sound of life over her sledgehammer pulse and burning lungs. But there is only silence below Jenkins's distant bellows, the woods swallowing her back into its threatening void.

Eve hides for hours in brush, behind trees, wherever she can find cover. She watches the sun rise overhead and then slowly sink into the sky again.

By the time night falls, Eve knows she has to move, or she will freeze to death. She runs until she is certain she will collapse.

Eventually, she breaks through the tree line, staggering into a moonlit clearing. Chest heaving, she scans for any signs of refuge, but finds only more woods enclosing her like a noose. She tries to go on, but her legs give way and she collapses, sobbing to the icy ground. Jenkins has run her to the ground for the final time.

Still, Eve refuses to give up. She forces herself up, and she reaches the road, but even that proves to be futile. A passing car does not see her, driving far too fast to notice her small figure reaching out from the tree line.

Meanwhile, Jenkins has closed in, his footsteps thudding closer through the dead leaves. Eve can barely lift her head, her throat too parched for useless pleas. Jenkins's shadow soon engulfs her limp form before his hands seize her arms and legs, lifting her like a rag doll.

"No more running, sweetheart," he rasps, his words slithering like a serpent. "Let's go home."

Jenkins slings Eve over his shoulder as he treks toward the cabin in the distance. Eve watches the bare tree branches recede above through tear-stung eyes. How long before she finds herself handcuffed to that bed once more, waiting for Jenkins's grinning face to appear each morning? Perhaps tomorrow Eve will not wake at all...perhaps that would be a blessing.

She thinks of Scott, of her family, and finally Eve's drifting gaze fixes upon the hunting knife handle glinting at his belt, smoothed by years of use. The polished steel winks at her like a hidden ally. As long as that blade remains inches from her grasping fingers, hope remains.

When Jenkins places her on the ground and drags her, Eve lets her body go limp, hearing his breath shorten with effort. Then Eve makes her move. She drives her elbow into his ear before grasping for the knife. Her frozen fingers close around the familiar leather.

Eve braces for him to charge, unsure if she can wield the knife with her drained muscles. But Jenkins only chuckles then, a slow grin spreading across his face.

"So, you want to play rough now? I taught you well, girl."

He takes one step toward Eve, then another. Eve wants to run, her wide eyes transfixed on his hulking form, but her quivering legs stand rooted. She holds the knife with both hands as he closes the distance.

"Please..." croaks Eve, almost unfamiliar to her own ears. "Don't."

Jenkins only sneers wider. He lunges for the blade.

Eve slashes out, feeling the knife catch flesh. Jenkins roars, clutching his forearm where a red gash runs from wrist to elbow. Black blood oozes down his coat sleeve, steaming in the frigid air. The sight of those dark rivulets brings Eve savage strength.

With animal speed, Jenkins launches himself toward Eve,

firing punches from his uninjured arm. Eve dances backward, swiping with the long hunting knife to keep distance between them. But the attacks force Eve to give ground. Soon her back hits against rough bark—a towering evergreen looms over her, cutting off escape.

Seeing Eve cornered, Jenkins presses his advantage, trying to barrel inside her guard to knock the knife loose. Eve ducks a punch, then plunges the knife into Jenkins's thigh, wrenching it back out in a fountain of hot blood. He crashes to his knees with a scream of agony, face contorting with pain and rage.

"You bitch!" he spits through gritted teeth. "I'll gut you for that..."

Eve knows she must finish this now, while hobbled. She leaps forward, meaning to drive the long knife into his chest. But Jenkins catches her wrist mid-blow with one massive hand, arresting the downward strike inches from his heart. His raw strength stuns Eve as iron fingers grind the delicate bones of her wrist, forcing her to her knees. She cries out, unable to wrench free as Jenkins bends her hand back, the knife lowered toward her own throat.

With his other fist, Jenkins fires punishing blows to Eve's face and body. Each punch lands like a sledgehammer, darkening her vision. Eve claws desperately at Jenkins's restraining arm with her free hand, but his corded muscles are like stone. As the knife edges closer to her hammering pulse, Eve goes limp, feigning unconsciousness.

Jenkins hesitates, the pressure easing for just a moment—long enough for Eve to strike. She drives stiffened fingers into his eye socket, then twists with all her might. Jenkins howls, reflexively releasing her wrist to grab for his ruptured eye.

In the same motion, Eve rips the knife back and plunges it to the hilt into Jenkins's chest, just left of his sternum. His bellow cuts off with a choking gurgle. Eve puts the last ounce of her weight behind the blade, forcing it deeper into muscle and sinew. She meets Jenkins's remaining wide eye.

"Never again," Eve hisses through bloodied teeth.

Jenkins shudders, dark blood pooling onto the ground beneath him. The towering menace who had tortured Eve for so long finally collapses sideways on the frozen ground. His limbs twitch, then go still.

Gasping violently, Eve drops the slick knife and staggers free of Jenkins's body. Is he really dead? Hugging herself, she scans the woods for any sign of life. But the forest remains eerily silent, save for the pounding of Eve's heart in her ears.

Through slowly bruising eyes, Eve regards the lifeless body of the man who had inflicted so much suffering. In his waning moments, Jenkins almost appears pitiful...small. Letting out an anguished sob, Eve turns from the clearing and trudges toward the country road without looking back.

39

Eve bursts from the tree line and collapses onto blessed asphalt. Every inch of her battered body screams for respite, but the two-lane country road beckons her onward — away from that damnable cabin, away from Jenkins's butchered body.

She bends at the knee, catching her breath, and when she has, she blinks up at the night sky's expanse, lit by a full moon. How long has it been since she gazed up at the stars? Their luminescence makes her want to weep. But she has not survived this hell just to die freezing on some forgotten road. Groaning, Eve drags her tortured frame upright and limps onward through the darkness.

The frigid air bites at Eve's skin through her tattered clothes, but that icy sting helps distract from the throbbing agony pulsating through her. In the silvery moonlight, every shredded inch of her stands out in stark relief—feet stripped raw and oozing inside what remains of her socks, bruised and bloodied fingers curled into claws, locks of filthy hair plastered to her face by sweat and blood...and the inky evidence of Jenkins's gruesome end coating her entire body.

As Eve shuffles along like a resurrected corpse, the events from that clearing keep replaying in her mind—Jenkins leering and pinned like a bug beneath her, the resistance of his flesh as she drove the knife home, the light fading from his eyes. Bile rises in her throat, but she forces it back down.

A memory creeps up, a phantom chill from Jenkins's roaming hands brushes over her, but Eve shakes it off, gritting her teeth. He will never touch her again.

The hysterical revelation ignites such intense relief that Eve finds herself laughing manically between wretched sobs. Passersby would surely think she has lost her mind, and maybe she has.

As if conjured by that thought, distant headlights cut through the darkness. Adrenaline overriding her pain, Eve lurches toward the approaching car like a marionette controlled by some demented puppeteer. Escape is within reach. She waves her arms, not caring what a sight she must be.

But as the car nears, her frenzied hope sinks—it's not slowing down. "Stop!" Eve shrieks, her voice ripping from her throat like rusted barbed wire. The vehicle cruises past as if she doesn't exist.

"Seriously?" Eve screeches after the shrinking taillights. Watching her salvation yet again speed off into oblivion snuffs out her last scrap of fortitude. She sinks to her knees at the road's edge, every injury, violation, and indignity crashing over her like a tidal wave. Is this how she dies after all—split open at the edges next to some godforsaken road, so very close to freedom?

Eve isn't sure if it's a sob or a laugh that escapes her lips as she resigns herself to a fate more twisted than even Jenkins could have devised. But then another engine rumbles from the darkness.

Headlights cut through the trees as an SUV rounds the bend. Eve thinks of Mira and of the boy back at that house, and so she gathers the very last dregs of her strength and rises on trembling legs, determined to end this once and for all. She lurches into the middle of the road, arms waving wildly.

The SUV slows then stops mere feet away, idling, as if wary of running her down. Escape is so close now Eve can practically taste it dancing on her tongue.

"Help..." she rasps, staggering those last few steps and splaying her palms on the vehicle's hood—a blessed altar of warmth and safety. Through the windshield, a family stares back in horror, faces waxen in the dashboard light. Two small children with matching gaped mouths...a father with thick-rimmed black glasses staring at her from behind the wheel...a wide-eyed mother raising a hesitant hand to her throat.

Their expressions scream louder than words. But none make a move to help her.

A ragged sob escapes Eve's cracked lips. Can she blame them? She must resemble every horror movie villain rolled together—the crazed ax murderer stumbling out of the woods to terrorize hapless motorists. If she were in their position, she would have locked the doors and gunned the gas pedal long ago.

But their stunned paralysis presents an opportunity, if Eve can just pacify them. Plastering her most non-threatening smile across her battered face, she croaks, "Please...help." Without breaking that surely grotesque grimace, she raises her hands and takes one small step back.

The family remains frozen, squinting through the windshield as if trying to rationalize away this midnight monster seeking refuge. Eve waits, dripping blood patiently onto pristine chrome. She considers smashing through the glass to let herself in but resists the urge. *You're so close now... just a few magic words are all it will take to finally escape this nightmare. What would a normal, unassuming victim say to them?*

"I..." Eve starts slowly, tasting each syllable like a fine wine. "I've been assaulted. He had a knife, but somehow, I got away." There—eerily calm while establishing herself as prey.

The father and mother share a hesitant glance. Their expressions soften by the barest degree. *It's working.* Eve presses on.

"Please, you have to help me. I think he might still be chasing me...." She lets her voice tremble, wide eyes beseeching. Never mind that her pursuer lies cooling in a forest clearing with a knife buried in his chest. They don't need those messy details now.

Decision made, the father puts the SUV in park and opens the driver's side door. "Okay, hop in back and we'll get you some help." Eve could cry from relief. Instead, she murmurs her thanks and circles the vehicle on leaden legs. Her frozen fingers close around the door handle like a lifeline. It swings open.

Sanctuary at last.

Some distant part of Eve's mind acknowledges she is ruining the pristine leather interior as she collapses onto the seat—bloody, dirt-encrusted clothes leaving rusty streaks across tan fabric. But she can't bring herself to care, not when heavenly warmth now washes over her.

Safe from the deadly cold, the family's muted voices, and the gentle rumble of tires over asphalt lull Eve toward much longed-for oblivion. But just before she surrenders to that siren call, an errant thought pierces through her foggy mind.

I never told them where to go...

Eve's eyes fly open, pulse hammering against her ribs once more. It's a long shot, but at this point, anything seems possible.

The parents murmur between themselves, paying their gruesome passenger no mind. Eve scrambles to pull her fractured wits together. She should tell them about the nearest hospital, or police station, or...

But her throbbing head refuses to dredge up any helpful information. Were they even headed toward town? Eve tries craning her neck to peer out the windows, but it's all darkness and trees flying past.

Panic sets in as Eve accepts the hard truth—she has willingly let strangers take her to parts unknown.

Eve meets her own horrified gaze reflected in the window.

After everything she's endured, a terrifying thought crosses her mind...what if she's just found a fate worse than Jenkins's cabin?

Thankfully, she hadn't.

Later, in the hospital, Eve wakes, drifting in and out of consciousness, her battered body and mind needing time to mend. When she finally awakens clear-headed, she looks up to see Scott sitting at her bedside, his concerned expression like a beam of sunlight penetrating the dark memories haunting her.

"You're awake," he says, grasping her hand. "The doctors said it's a miracle you survived out there as long as you did."

Eve manages a weak smile in return. There are so many things she wants to say...but only one thing bubbles to the surface.

"Mira and the boy...*Charlie*... did they find them?"

Scott nods, relief flooding his face. "Yes, after you told the cops where to search, they found Mira and Charlie still locked inside the house, too terrified to try escaping on their own. But they're safe now, thanks to you."

Overwhelming relief washes over Eve. She lays back, allowing her body to rest. They are safe. Their captor is dead. And she is finally free to start piecing her life back together.

Or so she thought.

40

Scott watches Eve's eyelids flutter open. His heart leaps—then sinks at the hollowness in her gaze. So much has transpired from the time Reed called to say they'd found Eve, to now, when she was finally awake and alert enough to talk.

"Eve." He surges forward, crushing her frail body in his arms. She tenses, then relaxes into the embrace.

After a long moment, he pulls back to search her face. "I need you to tell me what's going on..."

One look at her expression causes the world to tilt on its axis. Scott knows that no matter what might come out of Eve's mouth next, that the accusations against his wife are true.

She swallows hard. "What do you mean?"

"Morris says you arranged your own kidnapping...please tell me that's not true..."

Eve turns away, staring at the IV needle taped to her bruised arm. Her silence is answer enough.

Scott swallows hard. "I don't understand. How could you keep this from me? I thought I knew you." His voice cracks. "Who are you, really?"

"I wanted to tell you, I swear. But they threatened—"

"Who threatened you?" He grips her shoulders, fingers digging into bone, wanting her to tell him it's all lies, what the police and the media, what everyone is saying. "Dammit, Eve, talk to me!"

She flinches, eyes sliding away again. When she speaks, her tone is dull and distant. "I was trying to get my parents to hand over my trust fund. It got out of control."

"You're not serious?"

"I know it sounds crazy." Her gaze flickers to his for a second, dark and depthless as a cave. "You wouldn't understand."

He releases her and turns away, pressing the heels of his hands against his eyes. His wife, the person he thought he knew best, is merely another stranger with too many secrets.

After a long, leaden silence, he rasps, "Just tell me one thing… why didn't you trust me enough to tell me the truth?"

Eve's reply comes soft as a death rattle. "Because I didn't want to hurt you."

Scott shudders. He doesn't dare look at her, doesn't dare contemplate the abysmal darkness or the irony in her words.

Eve curls into herself, clutching the hospital blanket as if it could shield her from the wreckage of what was about to happen.

"I'm so sorry," she whispers. "I never meant to hurt you. I thought I could handle it. I—I thought I could just get the money…and everything would be okay…but I was wrong. I was so, so wrong. I never imagined it would turn out like this." Her voice hitches on a sob. "Please forgive me…"

Scott stands motionless, gaze fixed on the wall. He grapples for words, but finds none.

At last, he says tonelessly, "You should rest. We'll...we'll talk later."

He moves toward the door on wooden legs.

"Scott, please don't go—" Her plea echoes after him into the hall, frail and tremulous as the cry of a wounded animal. "I need you. I'm scared. You don't know what I've been through. You don't know the whole truth."

His step falters, and for an instant he hesitates on the threshold. But in the end, he keeps walking.

When the door clicks shut behind him, Scott slumps against the wall outside Eve's room, eyes squeezed shut. Everyone tried to tell him. They said run. They said do not marry her. She's a snake. He thought they were jealous, small-minded people who could never possibly understand. But now…

The cheerful, vibrant woman he thought he'd married is gone, replaced by this haunted shell of a person clinging to shadows and lies. He wants nothing more than to comfort her, to banish the ghosts that lurk behind her eyes—but how can he reach her when she won't tell him the truth?

With a sigh, he pushes off from the wall and starts down the hall. The soles of his shoes squeak on the polished floor, an abrasive sound scoring his frayed nerves.

By the time he reaches the lobby, he's made up his mind. He won't abandon Eve. At least not yet.

Scott strides back to her room, jaw set in grim determination. At the threshold he pauses, steeling himself, then steps inside.

Eve startles upright, eyes wide and wounded. "You came back." Her voice is small, fragile with hope.

"You're my wife," he says simply. "Where else would I go?"

Her lower lip trembles. She reaches for him in silent entreaty, and he crosses the room to take her hand.

"Tell me," he says, gaze steady on hers. "Tell me everything. I need to know."

Eve squeezes his hand, tears spilling down her cheeks. She draws a breath, ragged but resolute.

And she begins to speak.

41

Lucy raids the wine cellar for her parents' most expensive, most treasured bottle. It's not even noon, and she already needs a drink if she has to keep enduring this circus. Storming into the dining room, she pours herself a generous glass of Cabernet before dropping onto a satin settee.

Moments later, her parents blow into the room mid-argument, as usual.

"Honestly, Charles, I don't know why you insist on being so hard on the girl after all she's endured," her mother snaps, folding her arms.

Father drags a hand over his face, exhaustion etched in the lines around his eyes. "Elizabeth, our daughter has just admitted to faking her own abduction, which diverted countless resources and created needless panic. I think being 'hard on her' is more than warranted."

"She's clearly been through an ordeal, even if parts were...mischaracterized," her mother replies, lifting her nose. "We simply need to get Eve some help while keeping the family name out of any more embarrassing headlines."

Lucy loudly clears her throat before taking an aggressive gulp of wine. Honestly, if she has to choke down any more of their insipid bickering today...

"Did it ever occur to either of you that Eve is just an attention-starved brat?" Lucy snaps. "Because that's exactly what she is. And now, thanks to her little stunt, I missed my audition for the Broadway play, which I was GUARANTEED to land."

"Lucy, language," her mother tuts, though the reproach lacks any heat. She smooths back her impeccable blonde bob. "This family has endured quite enough scandal without my daughters squabbling like heathens."

Her father pinches his nose, glancing between Lucy and his wife. "Elizabeth, please..."

"Oh, don't 'Elizabeth, please' me, Charles," she retorts, gray eyes flashing. "Need I remind you that our family name just narrowly avoided being sullied by Eve's foolishness? The reporters are circling like vultures."

"Which is why discipline must be exercised, though it pains me to punish someone so clearly disturbed," Father replies. He turns to Lucy, features softening. "Don't worry, love. I intend to get Eve all the help she needs...discreetly. In the meantime, let's get you a nicer car to make up for this mess, hmm?"

Lucy hides her eye roll behind her wine glass. Of course, her father wants to buy his way out of emotional confrontation. She stands abruptly, schemes churning.

"I just want my sister back, Father," Lucy lies, injecting a wobble into her voice. "We have to help her, no matter what."

As expected, her parents trip over themselves to comfort their eldest daughter, the family's treasure. Lucy suppresses a twisted smile. She'll one-up her sister, all right. And permanently earn her rightful place in the spotlight. It's just a matter of time. The way it's always been.

42

Tears streak Eve's cheeks, her swollen eyes avoiding Scott's gaze. She takes a shaky pause, her chest heaving with emotion.

"What they are saying is true...I lied about everything. The abduction, the ransom—it was all staged. I contacted a group on the dark web that organizes extreme roleplaying scenarios. But I had no idea I was walking into a trap—that I was falling into the hands of a psychopath."

Eve's stomach churns as she forces the words out. "They advertise 'ultimate lifelike escapes' for people who want to experience danger and confinement without real risk. I paid them to abduct me so I could get money from my family."

Scott stares at her, eyes icy chips of blue. The vein in his temple throbs. "You mean to tell me this was some kind of twisted game to you?"

"No, I—I needed the money. I deserve my trust fund, and this was the only way—"

"The only way? Are you insane?" Scott throws his hands in the air. Eve flinches. "You could have been killed because of your idiotic scheme! I assaulted a man, Eve. I came close to throwing my whole life away for your sick, pathetic games. You had yourself kidnapped for ransom. You nearly died. And for what—all because I couldn't afford your lifestyle?"

"I didn't think it would be like that. I never imagined being in a situation like that man put me through..."

"What *did* you expect, Eve? A five-star hotel?"

Eve blinks back tears, her throat tightening. She turns her head so Scott won't see her cry. She knows she deserves his rage, his disgust.

"I'm so sorry," she whispers. "I was desperate and foolish and damaged in ways I never wanted you to see. I just wanted the money. I didn't grow up like this. I'm not used to being broke."

"Funny, that coming from you. I didn't realize how bankrupt you were—morally and emotionally. Money can't fix that."

Eve breaks down, weeping into her palms. When she can form words again, she begs. She pleads. She makes herself look small and pathetic, which is exactly how she feels. "I love you, Scott, and if you give me another chance, I swear I'll spend my whole life making this up to you. We can start over, be happy again—"

"Happy?" Scott shakes his head. "I don't even know who you are anymore. And I'm beginning to realize that maybe I never did. You humiliated me. They made me suspect number one. Do you know what that's like?"

Eve crumples, sobs racking her body. She reaches for Scott, but he pulls away.

"Leave me alone," he says. There is no anger left in his voice, only a bone-deep weariness. "I can't believe I actually fucking cared."

Eve staggers to her feet, wiping her eyes. She has lost him, she knows. The love that brought them together has shattered into jagged pieces beyond repair.

Scott turns and strides out of the hospital room, the door swinging shut behind him with finality.

Exhausted from the confrontation, Eve eventually cries herself to sleep.

Sometime later, she is jolted awake by the sound of the door opening. Still groggy, she assumes it's a nurse coming to check on her.

"Scott?" she croaks, squinting into the dim room.

A dark figure detaches from the shadows by the door. Eve's heart leaps into her throat. This is not Scott.

The stranger moves toward her bed. Eve shrinks back against her pillows. "Who are you? What do you want?"

A hand clamps over her mouth. Eve's screams die in her throat. She thrashes wildly, but her attacker's grip is a vise.

Searing words scorch her ear as a sinister voice whispers, "Don't say a word about us, Eve. Watch your back. Don't forget...we're always watching..."

The threat hangs heavy as her attacker releases her. Eve whirls around, but only empty space greets her.

Eve wakes with a start.

She lies shaking in the dark, breaths coming in ragged gasps. Her pulse pounds in her ears. She strains to peer into the shadows, searching for any sign of movement, but finds none. It was just another nightmare.

Eve wraps her arms around herself, skin crawling. She feels exposed in the quiet hospital room, like a thousand eyes are peering from the darkness. Judging. Waiting.

43

The therapist's gaze probes like a scalpel. Eve squirms on the leather sofa, mascara-streaked cheeks burning. She's always hated therapy, but now it's not just her parents insisting. It's her attorney too. She recalls the first time Scott learned about Dr. Walker, how confused he was. Eve feels sad realizing how little he actually knew. But how can you tell someone something they can't hear? It starts out as a whisper and then it becomes a scream, and now here they are. With Eve on a therapist's couch, and Scott ignoring her calls.

"Why did you orchestrate your own kidnapping?" Dr. Walker asks, leaning forward.

Eve's throat tightens. She pictures twisting the knife into Jenkins, him writhing from side to side. The memory ignites a sick thrill. She recoils at herself, pulse racing.

How did she become this monster?

Eve says, "I felt...entitled. To the money, the life I wanted. I convinced myself the ends justified the means."

"You were willing to put your loved ones through hell for money and thrills."

Eve cringes. She deserves the condemnation. A part of her

welcomes it. Finally, someone calling her out for not being the essence of perfection everyone else around her sees. "You tell me. You're the one who diagnosed me with narcissistic personality disorder."

Dr. Walker shakes her head, eyes softening. "Yes, but this is a new development, Eve. This is…well, this is a lot to take in. Even for you."

"Is it?"

"Your actions speak of a deep inner fracture. A demand for control and intensity that eclipsed empathy."

Eve's breath hitches. The diagnosis slices to her core. Maybe this is what she's always wanted. The truth about who she is.

"When did this fracture first emerge?" Dr. Walker asks gently.

They've been through all of this. But how else is Eve supposed to pass the next forty-seven minutes?

Childhood flickers through Eve's mind. Her father's ruthless business practices. Her parents' lavish parties. Their cold ambition and neglect. Her desperation for their notice. The dangerous thrill of deceiving them.

Eve whispers, "Maybe it was always there. Maybe I'm just...broken."

Dr. Walker grips her hand. "You're not broken, Eve. But you do have issues that require work. Rigorous honesty. Accountability for your actions. Learning empathy."

Eve squeezes her eyes shut, tears slipping free. "Maybe some people don't have the capacity for empathy."

She opens her eyes. Dr. Walker regards her with compassion. "Do you really believe that?"

"Yes, I just lived it."

"Did you ever consider...less extreme methods?" Dr. Walker asks, her brow furrowed.

"Of course," Eve snaps, her usual wit cutting through the despair. "But nothing could match the thrill, the power I felt when I set the plan in motion. Or relief." She pauses, realizing how twisted her desires had become. "I was so consumed by my desire to get what I wanted that I didn't care who I hurt."

As the implications settle in, the enormity of her actions hits her like a tidal wave. Eve sobs, her body racked with guilt and shame. Dr. Walker remains silent, allowing her patient the space to confront her demons, perhaps not realizing, *nor* caring, that it may all be an act.

Eve says quietly, "My whole life has felt like a performance. For my parents, friends, Scott... I got lost in the role I was playing."

"You felt unseen. Like your true self didn't matter."

Eve nods. "I chased bigger thrills to feel alive. When I couldn't get attention honestly, I'd lie or manipulate. Anything to provoke a reaction."

"You were desperate for validation and control. At the expense of empathy for how you impacted others."

Shame washes over Eve. She thinks of Scott's stricken face when he learned the truth.

"He loved me for who I was. But I couldn't accept that love. I kept pushing him away, betraying him, until..." Her voice breaks.

"Until your self-destruction became literal," Dr. Walker says gently.

Eve whispers, "He deserved so much better than me."

"Perhaps. But that doesn't mean you're undeserving of love. Or that you can't change."

“People don’t change,” Eve says. “Not really.”

"I do feel guilty for what I did to Scott," Eve adds. “Part of me knows it was wrong to deceive him like that. I do feel bad, but part of it was his fault. He married me without really even *knowing* me. He didn’t even know I was seeing you. All this time it was right under his nose. He couldn’t see it.”

Dr. Walker nods. "Go on."

“I don’t like not being seen. But let's be real, I'm not going to face any actual consequences," Eve continues casually. "My father has hired the best lawyers money can buy. He says the charges will disappear, and I'll never see a day in jail."

"I see," Dr. Walker says. "And how do you feel about that?"

Eve shrugs. "I'm relieved. Scott will never forgive me, but at least I won't be punished."

She pauses, playing with a thread on her sleeve. "What was shocking is realizing my own greed drove my scheme. I just wanted what I felt I deserved."

Dr. Walker frowns. "That type of ruthlessness can be dangerous, Eve."

"No one knows that better than me now," Eve replies. "But my father actually praised me for being so determined. He said now that he's seen my ruthless side, I'm ready to take over the family business since I've proven I'll do whatever it takes to get what I want."

Dr. Walker's eyes widen slightly. "And...how did that make you feel?"

"Proud," Eve admits. "Powerful. For once, my father saw me as worthy of my inheritance."

"Tell me more about that determination, Eve," Dr. Walker prompts, her voice gentle, yet firm.

Eve takes a shaky breath and meets her gaze. "I didn't even know it was there until...until I had my hands in its filthy grasp." Her words come out in a whisper, laced with horror and self-loathing. "It's like this evil twin, hiding in the shadows of my mind. And it pushed me to do despicable things."

"Can you trace back when that fracture began?" Dr. Walker asks, leaning forward. "When did this darkness—this *determination*—first take hold?"

"Are you looking for a new diagnosis, Doc? Multiple personality disorder?" Eve smirks. "Because the press would have a field day with that. And you know, it's not a half bad defense…."

"People with narcissistic personality disorder do not have multiple personalities. However, there are some aspects to how they present themselves that can make them seem as if they are totally different people from one moment to the next."

"Right."

"But what I asked was when you first felt the darkness you describe take hold."

Eve furrows her brow, her mind racing through years of memories, desperately searching for the root of it all. "I think...I think it started when I realized how easily I could manipulate people. How simple it was to twist their emotions…"

"Like a puppet master," Dr. Walker muses, her eyes narrowing with interest.

"Exactly," Eve agrees, her voice trembling. "But I never thought I'd go so far as to hurt the ones I love...to put their lives at risk just to secure my share of money."

"Sometimes," Dr. Walker says carefully, "our darkest desires can lead us down paths we never imagined possible. The important thing now is to confront those desires and understand what drove you to such extremes."

Eve nods, her heart pounding with a mix of fear and determination. "I want to change, Doc. I want to be free of this…this *darkness,* but I don't know how. I don't know if it's even possible."

"Nothing is impossible, Eve," Dr. Walker says, her voice steady and comforting.

But Eve knows it's a lie. Dr. Walker may believe what she's saying, but only because her father is paying her a hefty hourly rate to make it so.

Eve smiles. "That's what Dad always says."

44

The door slams with a resounding crash that echoes through the entire house. Scott stands motionless in the foyer, fists clenched at his sides. His heart hardens like stone at the thought of Eve's betrayal, leaving no room for forgiveness or second chances.

Eve rushes down the stairs, mascara streaming down her cheeks in black rivulets. She falls to her knees before Scott, grasping desperately at his pant legs.

"Please, you have to listen to me!" she sobs. "I never meant to hurt you. I'll do anything, be anything you want—just please don't leave!"

Scott looks down at her crumpled form. Her words ring hollow in his ears now. This isn't the strong, defiant woman he married. This is a pathetic stranger groveling at his feet.

He clenches his jaw, his expression resolute. With detached precision, he pries her fingers from his clothing. She collapses forward with a wail, palms slapping against the cold tile.

"We're through, Eve. The papers are signed."

Scott steps over her shaking body and walks out the front door without a backward glance.

He strides rapidly to his truck, jaw clenched. His pulse thrums as he forces himself not to turn back. There will be no forgiveness for what Eve has done. She betrayed their vows and destroyed his trust. Now he must cauterize this wound she inflicted on their lives, no matter how much it hurts.

He starts the engine and peels out down the street, putting distance between himself and the source of his agony. In the rearview mirror, he can see Eve sitting on the porch steps of what he once believed to be their happy home, calling him back like a siren on the rocks. He hardens his heart, resolve settling into his bones, and drives on. Eve made her choice—now he must make his.

45

Eve stares at the taillights of Scott's truck as he drives away, chest hollow, as the reality sinks in. It's over. He's really leaving her. Panic bubbles up inside, writhing and twisting, shredding the last tethers of her control.

No. He can't leave. He's hers.

The divorce papers burn in her hands, a physical manifestation of all her ruined hopes and dreams. She pictured a perfect life with Scott, a cozy house and laughter-filled dinners. Family vacations and growing old together.

Now those idyllic visions lay shattered at her feet, destroyed by her own hands. Her lies, her deceits, her selfishness. She drove him away at last.

As the full impact hits her, a sob rises in her throat. She leans back against the house as ragged, choking cries burst out of her.

She stays there for hours, drowning in her grief. When darkness falls, she finally picks herself up, eyes rimmed red but purpose igniting in her chest.

She failed to keep Scott, the one bright light in her bleak existence. But she won't lose anything else.

Inside, she makes a beeline for the liquor cabinet, her resolve hardening into something twisted and unrecognizable. She'll keep her secrets, her control, her hollow little world.

No one else is leaving her. Not if she has anything to say about it.

But for now, she drinks until the living room spins around her. She braces herself against the back of the couch as a fresh wave of sobs racks her body. Gasping, she claws open the liquor cabinet and fishes out another unopened bottle of vodka.

With trembling hands, Eve unscrews the cap, not even bothering with a glass. She lifts the bottle to her lips and chugs, the harsh liquid burning her throat. But the pain is nothing compared to the gaping void inside her.

She drops onto the sofa, vodka sloshing. The room blurs around the edges as she continues drinking like it's the elixir of life itself. Maybe if she lets oblivion consume her, her heart will stop aching. Eve hates to lose.

She knows there are only a few places Scott could have retreated to, and she plans to check every one of them.

But then her phone rings, and she sees her father's name on the screen. He can tell Eve has been crying. "Come on now," he says. "Remember that song, the one I always played for you when you were little?"

Eve sniffles and wipes her nose with the back of her hand. "'Hell's Bells?'"

Her dad laughs. "No. 'Cowgirls Don't Cry.'"

"But I'm not a cowgirl, Dad. I'm really not."

"You're whatever you want to be, darling. Now go wash your face and give Victor a call. He's expecting you."

46

Lucy slams the front door hard enough to rattle the entryway frame. The nerve of that stupid detective to suggest Eve's return is something to celebrate! As if her pathetic sister hadn't just wasted thousands of taxpayer dollars and manpower hours on her little attention-seeking ploy.

Storming upstairs to her bedroom, Lucy slings her designer handbag onto her duvet. Of course, Mommy and Daddy believe Eve's absurd story about escaping some psycho kidnapper in the woods. The way they fawn over their poor wounded baby girl is enough to make Lucy violently ill.

And the press just eats up her damsel-in-distress act! Her father may very well be paying them, but still. Lucy had turned on the TV, hoping for vindication, only to get slapped with more nausea-inducing coverage singing Eve's praises. Breaking news banner flashing, reporters gushing about the victim's "miraculous" rescue, police officials recounting Eve's "harrowing tale of survival." Sure, Eve staged her own abduction, but she never expected to fall into the hands of a sicko like Henry Jenkins.

Even when caught red-handed staging her own abduction, Eve

has somehow once again managed to worm her way into the heroic spotlight while Lucy burns in the background.

What could her precious sister have expected? As if you're sliding into the life of a moral and ethical person when someone offers to kidnap you for a cut of the money!

Lucy powers on her laptop. She should be the one fielding interview requests and giving tearful statements about getting her beloved sister back safely, not Eve soaking up more undeserved sympathy.

Well, Lucy refuses to let Eve's lies win. If the justice system wants to buy Eve's victim act, despite all the evidence to the contrary, Lucy will just need to seek vengeance through other means. She doesn't understand how her sister could be so stupid, unless of course, she wanted to get caught. Henry Jenkins was a stickler for record keeping. Not only did he have signed documents and evidence of wire transfers in his possession, he kept every correspondence that ever existed. And the authorities have it all.

Lucy vows that she will not be as reckless as Eve was. She will tie up her loose ends.

Her manicured nails tap as she logs into the shadow web forums—the only place that won't coddle her manipulative sister.

Maybe it's time to have another peek at those illegal poisons for sale on the dark web. Then dear Eve can finally retire the spotlight she seems so desperate for. Maybe she wouldn't actually go through with any of it, but she would certainly be playing on her sister's level. That would get her parents attention.

Lucy chuckles quietly, a subtle ripple of amusement escaping her lips. Yes, death might be the only way to upstage Eve's melodramatic tales at this point. Won't Mommy and Daddy have such fawning sympathy for their remaining precious daughter struck by tragedy? The prodigal screw-up roasted in effigy while the successful shining star receives her richly-deserved accolades.

A slow smile spreads across Lucy's face as she types out a new message to the shadow brokers and assassins lurking in darkness.

I have a problem I need permanently erased. Let's talk rates.

47

Eve sits at her desk, nibbling on the end of her pen as she tries to gather her thoughts. Her younger sister Lucy had finally gone too far, and now their parents have confined her to a fancy mental institution for the rich and disturbed.

Sunrise Hills Rehabilitation Center is the type of place only serious money can buy—more country club than asylum, with equine therapy, massage sessions, and gourmet vegan meals. The brochure boasts of a "holistic healing approach" but Eve knows the facility's real purpose is keeping trouble carefully hidden.

She sighs, twirling her hair around one finger. Lucy's venomous scheming has only grown more dangerous since Eve returned from her staged kidnapping. While Eve soaked up public sympathy as the traumatized victim, Lucy seethed at being upstaged yet again.

Eve shakes her head, thinking back to the night everything erupted. Lucy had been caught red-handed trying to hire a hitman online to solve her "Eve problem." For once, their parents could no longer ignore the twisted hatred consuming their younger daughter.

So now Lucy finds herself enjoying an involuntary stay at

Sunrise Hills, confined to the sprawling grounds while she undergoes intense therapy. And Eve has been tasked with spinning this latest family crisis to the media, portraying Lucy as a misguided but sympathetic victim of circumstances, which is a lot harder than it sounds.

No one will ever understand how much goes into trying to stay on top. Or how difficult family can be.

Eve walks into the opulent living room where her parents sit waiting. She chose an understated black dress for this difficult conversation, knowing her mother hates muted tones.

Her father glances up from his newspaper. “Well, what have you come up with for Lucy’s statement?”

Eve smooths her dress and sits across from them. “I have a draft addressing Lucy’s stay at the rehabilitation center.”

Her mother frowns in distaste. "Yes, Sunrise Hills Rehabilitation Center. It's a dreadful name, in my opinion. But I suppose we must do what is needed."

“We’ll say it’s for exhaustion,” Eve’s father declares. “Too many charity events and Broadway auditions. The poor dear just needs a rest.”

Eve shakes her head. “I don’t think that will contain this, not anymore. The authorities know what Lucy tried to do.”

Her mother waves a hand dismissively, diamonds glinting. “No need to dwell on it. Just say she had a mental break of some kind. Play up her fragility.”

Looking between them, Eve takes a moment to compose herself. “I think we should acknowledge Lucy needs help. How troubled she’s become trying to compete with me.”

Her father slaps his newspaper down. “And have the media vultures smearing the family name, implying we’re bad parents? I won’t allow it.”

“Admitting Lucy needs help isn’t a smear. Maybe it would help her, not having to pretend—”

“Oh Eve, enough.” Her mother sighs. “We all know you girls

aren't perfect. But we protect our own, whatever it takes. You, of all people, should understand that."

Eve resists the urge to vomit. "Perhaps we could try actual parenting for once instead of cover-ups?"

Her father snorts. "Please, that's what the staff at Sunrise Hills is for. Equine therapy, artisan cheese tastings—they'll have Lucy back to her charming, malicious self in no time."

He hands the statement back to Eve. "I'm sure you can come up with something appropriately saccharine. Lay it on thick, but no mention of murder plots. We have appearances to keep up."

Eve presses her lips together, considering. They're right—she has no room to expect Lucy to face her issues when her own mistakes were concealed. Lucy doesn't really want her dead. She just wants to win.

Finally, she nods. "You'll need to review the statement draft. I said Lucy is taking a sabbatical for wellness reasons, effective immediately. Vague but positive."

Her father relaxes back into his chair. "Good girl. Put a ribbon on it, and we'll move forward." He lifts his newspaper, scanning the financial section. "We have an image to maintain."

Eve's mother downs her scotch. "Your father is right, dear. We all know Lucy has been under strain. The pressure of living up to your impossible example would drive anyone mad." She refills her glass. "We simply need to tweak the wording, so Lucy still appears sympathetic. Like that Brooke woman who shot her lover. Temporary insanity, wasn't it?"

Eve stares down at the paper. She shouldn't be surprised—for this family, image always trumps reality, no matter how deranged. With a resigned smile, Eve heads off to rewrite Lucy's redemption story. After all, she owes them for covering up her own unscrupulous past. For better or worse, they're family.

48

The polished marble floors shone under Eve's stiletto heels as she strode through the lobby of her family's company headquarters. To the outside world, she was the picture of poise—hair coiffed just so, lips painted crimson, designer suit crisp and tailored. Inside, her stomach churns.

Only six months since the divorce, and here she was, about to step back into the viper's nest. Still, she forced her lips into a smile as she approached the front desk.

"Eve! So good to have you back," the receptionist chirps. Eve nods, her gaze already drifting toward the elevators. As the doors slide open, she slips inside, shoulders loosening once alone.

Up on the fortieth floor, Eve braces herself before pushing into her office.

"Welcome back, boss," her secretary greets her with a knowing look. Eve ignores it, striding past into the inner sanctum.

It's just as she left it two years ago, when she fled this life of cold marble and colder gazes. The ghost of her old self lingers here, hovering disapprovingly over the sleek desk and leather chair.

Eve sinks into it with a sigh, letting her eyes fall closed. Just a moment of peace before the vultures descend. She wakes hours later when a sharp rap at the door shatters the silence. Her secretary peeks in. "Mr. Roth is here for your lunch meeting."

Victor. Eve smooths the annoyance from her face as she rises to greet her suitor and most formidable adversary. Tall and impeccably dressed, he sweeps into the office, pressing a kiss to her cheek.

"Eve, darling. Shall we?" He gestures to the elevator, slipping an arm around her waist. Eve endures it with a gracious smile.

As the elevator doors close, sealing them in, Eve meets her own gaze in the polished metal. The woman staring back has flinty eyes—and a predator's smile.

Good, she thinks. She'll need that killer instinct if she's going to survive this place again. Her parents want her to marry Victor, the man the empire they've built demands, and at times seems to almost ride on it. She has said yes, for now. But only because she is in hot water and she needs the protection they provide.

The doors slide open to the restaurant on the top floor. Heads turn. Victor guides her forward into the lion's den.

Eve maintains her poise as they're seated at the finest table in the restaurant. Victor, ever the gentleman in public, holds her chair and smooths her napkin across her lap once she's settled. His hand lingers a moment too long on her thigh before withdrawing.

"I must say, it's a delight to see you back in the city, Eve," he says, signaling the waiter for a bottle of their best champagne. "I always knew you'd return to your rightful place."

Eve forces a smile, ignoring the undercurrent in his words. Her rightful place under his thumb, as just another prize in his glittering collection.

"Well, the family business called," she replies. "Duty before pleasure, as they say."

"All work and no play?" Victor tsks. "What a dreary existence. A woman like you should be adorned in the finest silks, lounging on yachts and in summer villas." His eyes drift down her figure. "I'd be happy to provide such a lifestyle, if you wished it."

Eve's smile doesn't falter, even as her skin crawls. "You're too kind, but I rather enjoy keeping busy."

His answering smile is razor sharp. "For now, perhaps. But you'll soon remember how tedious these...duties…can be." He reaches out to grasp her hand, running his thumb over her knuckles. "Luckily, I'm here to take some of that burden from your delicate shoulders."

Eve wants to recoil from his clammy touch, but she forces herself to endure it. This is just another kind of battlefield, with its own rules of engagement.

She meets Victor's hooded gaze. "You're very generous," she says. "I'm lucky to have you."

His fingers tighten possessively over hers. "Yes, you are."

Eve pulls her hand from Victor's grasp under the pretense of checking her watch. "Actually, I have to go. I've just realized I forgot about a meeting I must take. Raincheck on lunch?"

Victor's eyes flash, but his tone remains light. "Of course. Business before pleasure."

As Eve turns to leave, his hand darts out to seize her wrist. His grip is viselike, fingertips digging into her skin. She inhales sharply.

Victor steps closer, his voice an indistinct murmur meant only for her. "Don't forget, my dear. I decide when it's time for...pleasure."

His thumb caresses the inside of her wrist, right over her racing pulse. Eve forces herself to meet his gaze evenly, despite the revulsion churning inside her.

"I look forward to it," she says. The lie tastes bitter on her tongue.

Victor searches her face, then nods, appeased. "Until then." He releases her wrist and steps back, as if nothing had happened.

Eve walks to the elevator, head held high. But inside, she is trembling. Her skin still crawls from Victor's touch, his possessiveness. She had not escaped one monster only to end up ensnared by another. Absolutely not.

Eve smiles grimly to herself. Victor has no idea who he's dealing with. She will be no one's prize.

49

Eve watches Mira's hands trembling, as if the very air in the sleek high-rise office were electrified with old fears. They sit knee-to-knee on the modern leather chairs, the floor-to-ceiling windows looking out over the glimmering city, a testament to Eve's worldly success.

Mira's voice, fractured and brittle, rises like a specter from the abyss of her chest.

"Every night, he's there—Jenkins," Mira whispers, the name a shard of ice on her tongue. "Leering at me...from every shadow."

The office lights flicker briefly, casting brief dances of light and dark across Mira's face. Eve feels the shadows around them pulse with silent laughter, mocking their shared paranoia.

"Charlie's mom says he's okay, you know? But what's okay about any of this?" Mira's eyes are wide, lost pools reflecting Eve's own disquiet.

"Okay is overrated," Eve replies, the words carrying a sardonic twist she didn't quite intend. Mira doesn't smile, but there's a spark of something akin to humor in her gaze—an acknowledgment of the absurdity of their plight.

Eve stands, pacing the perimeter of the sleek office like a caged animal, scenting freedom through the bars. Her past—a collage of impulsive thrills chased and hollow victories—seems so distant now. "You're the only one who isn't mad at me about the little mishap with my kidnapping...why?"

"You mean that you staged it?"

"Well, when you put it like that, yes."

"You helped me. Even when you didn't have to. I probably would have been killed if not for you."

"I guess I'm still a little confused about how you and the boy ended up there. Is there anything you want to tell me, Mira? Anything you need to get off your chest."

"No."

Eve wonders for a split second whether Mira is lying. But then she thinks it's completely logical that Jenkins kidnapped her for no other reason than that he was a psychopath. After all, he did have all of those other girls in his garden. Surely, there can't be that many people out there like Eve? They couldn't all have been hired hits. Surely, there is room for *actual* crazy in the world. Eve thinks of what Scott said. It wasn't like she was hooking herself up with a moral and ethical person. Not when extortion is involved. And so, she believes Mira. Almost.

"You're right," Eve says. "You were lucky. It is actually quite common in places around the world, that even after a family pays ransom, they don't ever see their family member again. The kidnappers believe it's too risky and they are afraid of getting caught, ruining their business operation, so they just kill them. Thank God that wasn't you."

"My family has no money for ransom," Mira says. "But I don't think that's what Jenkins was after anyway..."

"Exactly. Which is why I'm going to help you," Eve declares, the conviction in her voice steadier than her racing heartbeat. "I'll get you the money and the resources to start a nonprofit—advocacy work—something to take your mind off things."

"You don't have to do that..."

"But I do. This is my chance—*our* chance—to turn things around."

"Your parents?" Mira's question hangs between them, fraught with doubt. "And Victor? I know how they feel about you looking back on all this…"

"They'll understand." It's a lie, sweet as poisoned honey. "Helping you might just be the one right thing left for me to do."

Mira nods, her gratitude a tangible warmth in the chill of the office. Eve feels it seep into her bones, a golden thread weaving through the tapestry of her fractured spirit. She is Eve, the fixer, the redeemer; for once not the catalyst of chaos, but the architect of someone else's salvation.

"Thank you," Mira says, and Eve can almost taste the irony. For all her persuasive charm and cunning, it took becoming someone's lifeline to glimpse her own humanity.

Eve sees Mira out, a soft smile crossing her face. Helping Mira heal has given Eve a renewed sense of purpose. For the first time in years, her own pain and darkness feel conquerable. She has something to look forward to.

Within minutes after Mira's departure, the office door swings open and Victor walks in. His face is stony.

"Who was that woman?" he asks sharply.

"Mira," Eve says lightly. "We were catching up."

"I thought I told you not to speak to her anymore." Victor's voice is cold.

Eve stiffens. "What right do you have to say who I can and can't talk to?"

Victor steps closer, looming over her. "Every right. And you know why. She's filling your head with dangerous ideas. Making you question things you shouldn't. She's trying to extort you… using your emotions to ply money and God knows what else out of you."

Eve shakes her head, backing away. "That's ridiculous. Mira is my friend."

"You don't need friends like her. You have me." Victor grabs Eve's wrist, his fingers biting into her skin.

Eve tries to pull away. "Let go! You're hurting me."

Victor tightens his grip. "No more, Mira. No more "support" groups. No more of this 'healing' nonsense. You are my fiancée, and you'll do as I say."

Tears spring to Eve's eyes as she wrests her hand away. She cradles her wrist, blood pounding in her ears.

"What is wrong with you?"

Victor's face softens. He reaches out to caress her cheek. "Wrong? There's nothing wrong. I love you. But you don't know what's best for you. You need my guidance, my protection."

He kisses the top of her head. "You've always been such a fragile thing. Mira is only enabling your weakness, stopping you from facing your true self. But I know who you really are, what you really need."

Eve squeezes her eyes shut, trying to block him out. But she feels the rage rising within her once more.

She retreats to the bathroom off her office, closing the door softly behind her. She stands motionless, staring blankly as shadows creep across the walls.

Her mind churns, that familiar spiral of obsessive thoughts returning. If only she could silence them, quiet the tempest raging inside her. Sometimes—often—she can. But not today.

Eve sinks to the floor, hugging her knees. Rocking slowly back and forth, back and forth. She tries to remember the coping strategies Dr. Walker taught her, the mindfulness techniques. But they crumble away until only the obsessive thoughts remain, consuming her.

Maybe Victor is right. Maybe she is worthless. Useless. A burden to him, her parents, to everyone around her. She deserves to be locked away where her defective mind can't inflict itself upon the world.

Eve's rocking ceases as stillness settles over her…a strange calmness as she contemplates a permanent solution, a way to finally escape the prison of her own mind.

She eyes the amber prescription bottles in the medicine cabinet. Wonders how many it would take. Wonders if Victor would even care, or if he, too, would be relieved to have her silenced.

Eve stands abruptly. She can't stay here, trapped in this room with her poisonous thoughts. Grabbing her coat, she hurries to the elevator and out of the building, desperate to outrun the darkness threatening to swallow her whole.

The cold air hits Eve's face as she steps outside, but it does nothing to clear her cluttered mind. She wanders aimlessly down the sidewalk, no destination in mind. Just movement, as if she could physically leave her obsessive thoughts behind.

But they follow, relentless. *Worthless. Useless. Broken. Unlovable.* The words repeat like a broken record in her mind. She shakes her head violently, as if she could shake them loose, dislodge them completely. It doesn't work.

In her pocket, her phone buzzes. For a wild moment, hope leaps within her—could it be Mira reaching out? Or Scott? But no. The name flashing on her screen is 'Dead to me.' Lucy.

Eve hesitates, then answers.

"Eve!" Lucy's voice is bright and bubbly. "I've been thinking about you lately. How are you doing?"

Eve opens her mouth, but no words form. How can she begin to explain the mess inside her head?

"That good, huh?" Lucy gives a little laugh. "Listen, I'm out of that godforsaken place now…"

"I heard."

"You should come visit me here in Hawaii! A tropical vacation would be so good for you."

A vacation...the idea seems absurd. Eve tries to picture herself lounging on a beach next to a sister who doesn't even like her—who tried to have her killed. Impossible.

"I don't think so, Luce." Her voice comes out flat, emotionless. "I'm not really up for travel right now."

Lucy sighs dramatically. "You're never up for anything anymore! I'm worried about you, sis. You need to get out of your funk."

Get out of her funk. As if it were that simple, that easy. Anger coils hotly in Eve's gut. Lucy has spoken to Victor.

"You have no idea what I'm going through," she snaps. "But sure, a vacation will fix everything."

Eve ends the call abruptly, cutting off Lucy's squawk of protest. Her hands tremble with a mix of anger and shame.

Her heart hammers against her ribcage, a frenzied echo of footsteps pounding down an endless corridor in her mind. Sleep, once a sanctuary, now betrays her with dreams of flight. She imagines herself running toward a tall bridge, Victor's voice a thunderous god behind her, always behind her. Sometimes it's Jenkins. More often, it's Victor.

Now in the waking world, Eve finds her feet have carried her to the exact bridge featured in her recurring nightmare. Heart pounding, she approaches the railing under the bright daylight and looks over. The same inky water churns below, the same sick allure pulling her toward the edge.

Eve's chest tightens, reality blurring with the remnants of her dream. All it would take is one step, one leap into that void below. No more pain, no more torment. Just the siren song of the depths calling her home.

She places her hands on the railing, leaning forward. A horn blares in the distance, jolting Eve from her trance. She stumbles back, chest heaving.

Eve looks around dazed, realizing where she is and what she almost did. The sun glints off the passing cars, illuminating the tears on her cheeks. She's come so close to letting the darkness win.

Wrapping her arms around herself, she walks unsteadily away

from the bridge. Each step takes monumental effort, but she forces herself forward.

She has survived this battle, but the war still rages in her fragile mind. The bridge continues to call, its haunting song not fully silenced even in the light of day. As Eve brushes the tears away with the back of her hand, it's her father's voice she hears.

"Shake it off, kid. Even villains have bad days."

50

Eve's cursor hovers over the link, memories flooding back unbidden. The ad is still there after all this time, that shadowy promise of deliverance. She remembers the desperation that had driven her to it before, the gnawing fear that she would be forever poor. She's a different kind of poor now, and she'll never break free of Victor's grasp.

Eve glances over her shoulder, but Victor is still sleeping soundly in their bed. She shouldn't, she knows she shouldn't, and yet...

Eve clicks the link with trembling fingers, heart hammering in her chest. The screen blinks to a video call interface. This is crazy. Reckless. But the temptation consumes her thoughts like a sickness, the compulsion to reach out and grasp that slender thread of hope.

She tenses as the chat connects, revealing a face shrouded in darkness. "Well, well," a gravelly voice intones, "Eve. It's been a while."

Eve shudders at the sound of that voice, once her salvation, now the specter of her darkest impulses.

"Did you miss me?" The silhouette grins coldly.

Eve grips the mouse, poised on the brink. The past calls to her, but the future awaits her response.

Eve's hand trembles, the mouse hovering over the disconnect button. She should end this madness now, sever this tie to her troubled past once and for all.

But the voice on the screen has a sinister allure, promising deliverance with its sibilant whispers.

"What's wrong, Eve?" the voice croons. "Don't you want to be free of him?"

Eve's eyes dart again to Victor's sleeping form. Yes, she wants her freedom desperately. But she recoils from the cold brutality implied by that eerie voice.

"I've changed," Eve says. "I won't compromise who I am, not even for your so-called freedom."

“Come now, we both know that isn’t true,” the voice insists. “Besides, we've missed you...”

Eve silences the voice with a decisive click, ending the chat. Her hand still shakes, partly from fear but also from defiance. She has faced her demons and prevailed. With newfound resolve, Eve closes the laptop. She will find another way, without sacrificing her soul. The past is dead to her now. It is time to turn the page.

Eve sits back, a tremor running through her. She has resisted the temptation to contact her shadowy "friends" once more. But the yearning still pulls at her, a different version of the siren song. This one pure danger and deliverance.

She glances over at Victor's sleeping form. Repulsion and rage simmer within her. How she hates being confined here, subjected to his control and delusions. She longs to break free, by any means necessary.

Eve turns her gaze to the laptop screen, now dark. Her finger hovers over the power button, tempted to reboot it and reconnect.

Just one click away lies potential escape. The thrilling promise of outwitting her fiancé and vanishing into the night calls to Eve like a drug. If only it had gone differently before...

Eve balls her hand into a fist, fighting the compulsion. It would be so easy to slip back into darkness. But she has vowed to find another way.

Still...perhaps she could contact them just one last time. Strictly for information, no commitments. What could it hurt?

Eve's finger drifts toward the keyboard.

"What's wrong, Eve?" the voice croons. "You couldn't stay away?"

"Something like that."

"So, you want to be free of him?"

Eve's eyes dart again to Victor's sleeping form. Yes, is all she can think to say.

"I need you to take him off my hands," Eve says, her voice steady and unwavering despite the gravity of her request.

The dark figure chuckles. "Kidnapping? My dear, that will cost you."

Eve's stomach churns, but her resolve hardens. "Name your price. I'll pay anything to be rid of him."

They negotiate the details, Eve agreeing to a fee that at least partially drains her trust fund. Her hands shake, but she does not waver.

The arrangements made, Eve ends the chat with a decisive click. Her pulse races, but it is done—she has sealed Victor's fate.

Eve stares at the laptop. She sits back, with a stiff exhale. Eve couldn't resist slipping back into the darkness, but made the only choice she could see to secure her freedom.

Rising quietly, she moves to the small window. Somewhere beyond these walls, her liberation awaits. She will find it, even if it takes everything she has. It is time to turn the page.

Just as soon as Victor is taken care of, she'll reach out to Scott. Everyone tells her to leave well enough alone, but Eve does not like to lose, so of course she has to get Scott back. Or destroy his happiness if she can't.

She heard through the grapevine that he's dating again—that he has a girlfriend, possibly a serious one. But that's no problem. One click here, one click there.

Eve knows everything can be fixed.

A NOTE FROM BRITNEY

Dear Reader,

I hope you enjoyed reading *I Said Run.*

Writing a book is an interesting adventure, it's a bit like inviting people into your brain to rummage around. *Look where my imagination took me. These are the kind of stories I like...*

That feeling is often intense and unforgettable. And mostly, a ton of fun.

With that in mind—thank you again for reading my work. I don't have the backing or the advertising dollars of big publishing, but hopefully I have something better...readers who like the same kind of stories I do. If you are one of them, please share with your friends and consider helping out by doing one (or both) of these quick things:

1. Visit the review page and write a 30 second review (even short ones make a big difference).

Many readers don't realize what a difference reviews make but they make ALL the difference.

2. If you'd like to make sure you don't miss anything, to receive an email whenever I release a new title, sign up for my new release newsletter.

(https://britneyking.com/new-release-alerts/)

Thanks for helping, and for reading my work. It means a lot.

Britney King

Austin, Texas

April 2024

ABOUT THE AUTHOR

Britney King lives in Austin, Texas with her husband, children, two very literary dogs, one ridiculous cat, and a partridge in a peach tree.

When she's not wrangling the things mentioned above, she writes psychological, domestic and romantic thrillers set in suburbia.

Without a doubt, she thinks connecting with readers is the best part of this gig. You can find Britney online here:

Email: hello@britneyking.com
Web: https://britneyking.com
Facebook: https://www.facebook.com/BritneyKingAuthor
TikTok: https://www.tiktok.com/@britneyking_
Instagram: https://www.instagram.com/britneyking_/
BookBub: https://www.bookbub.com/authors/britney-king
Goodreads: https://bit.ly/BritneyKingGoodreads
Newsletter: https://britneyking.com/newsletter/

Want to make sure you never miss a release? Sign up for Britney's newsletter: https://britneyking.com/newsletter/

Happy reading.

ACKNOWLEDGMENTS

Many thanks to my family and friends for your support in my creative endeavors.

To the beta team, ARC team, and the bloggers, thank you for making this gig so much fun.

Last, but not least, thank you for reading my work. Thanks for making this dream of mine come true.

I appreciate you.

ALSO BY BRITNEY KING

Standalone Novels

I Said Run

Blood, Sweat, and Desire

The Sickness

Ringman

Good and Gone

Mail Order Bride

Fever Dream

The Secretary

Passerby

Kill Me Tomorrow

Savage Row

The Book Doctor

Kill, Sleep, Repeat

Room 553

HER

Around The Bend

Series

The New Hope Series

The Social Affair | Book One

The Replacement Wife | Book Two

Speak of the Devil | Book Three

The New Hope Series Box Set

The Water Series

Water Under The Bridge | Book One

Dead In The Water | Book Two

Come Hell or High Water | Book Three

The Water Series Box Set

The Bedrock Series

Bedrock | Book One

Breaking Bedrock | Book Two

Beyond Bedrock | Book Three

The Bedrock Series Box Set

The With You Series

Somewhere With You | Book One

Anywhere With You | Book Two

The With You Series Box Set

****For a complete and up-to-date reading list please visit britneyking.com**

GET EXCLUSIVE MATERIAL

Looking for a bit of dark humor, chilling deception and enough suspense to keep you glued to the page? If so, visit britneyking.com to receive your free starter library. Easy peasy.

SNEAK PEEK: THE SICKNESS

Best-selling author Britney King returns with an adrenaline-fueled thriller about an unlikely array of characters and their heart-pounding plunge into the dizzying depths of madness.

March 2020: Stranded on a remote cruise ship as the pandemic ravages the world, 753 desperate passengers find themselves in a perilous situation. With no hope of docking in sight and dwindling supplies, each must fight their inner demons to survive. Among them are an eclectic mix of people—a father desperately searching for a way to save his daughter's future, an artist running from a broken past, and a hacker looking to make one last score. But what they didn't count on is the mysterious cult convention taking place on board.

With enough resources at stake to change or end lives, suspicion and fear quickly build. When bodies begin to drop, they question —is it the virus? Or is it one of them?

Don't miss this spine-tingling psychological thriller that takes readers on a white-knuckle ride to uncover the truth and find out who—*if any*—will make it off the ship alive.

COPYRIGHT

Hot Banana Press

Cover Design by Britney King LLC

Cover Image by Robert Thiem

Copy Editing by Librum Artis

Proofread by Proofreading by the Page

First Edition: 2023

ISBN 13: 9798215020630

ISBN 10: 8215020630

britneyking.com

THE SICKNESS

BRITNEY KING

“The road to hell is paved with good intentions.”

— Proverb

PROLOGUE

The world is spinning too fast for me to make any sense of it. Fear and desperation choke the air as a steady buzz of panicked whispers fill the background like static. The wind whips my hair across my face as I stand on the deck, the ocean crashing beneath me. A thousand eyes seem to be upon me.

My fellow passengers are in chaos, their faces wild and terror-stricken as they grab supplies and flee from the horror. The ship isn't as full as it once was, but it's still crowded, and people race in all directions, panic spreading like wildfire. Everywhere I look, people are in a state of desperation. Some run, some cower, and some simply stand frozen, as if waiting for the inevitable.

I search for Dad, and I feel my own panic rise within me. I see hundreds of faces, but none are his.

Then I hear him calling out my name.

"Abby!"

"Dad?"

"Abby!"

Finally, I spot him across the deck, arms full of water bottles, and I exhale the breath I'd been holding. He motions for me to move forward as planned, and I dash toward the bread line, thirst scratching at my throat after a full day without water. Over my shoulder, I watch my dad weave through the crowd. He has that same look on his face he had when he told me about this trip—determination mixed with dread—and I know what's going through his head: We should have never gotten on this ship.

Roger Atkins has never been a cruise ship kind of guy, but considering the circumstance, what could he say?

"It'll be an adventure, I guess," he'd finally said, and he was right.

"Next!" a woman shouts, and I move forward in line.

I hand over my ration card to a lady with dead eyes. Children aren't supposed to be on deck when rations are dispersed, but I'm not most children. I'm sixteen, though I might as well be eighty. People frequently utter words like "last resort" and "little hope" when they think I'm not listening. One look at me and it goes without saying.

I grab two loaves of bread and can't help the satisfied grin that washes over my face. We have water and we have bread. Everything is right in the world again. I glance toward my dad in triumph, but something else captures my eye.

An eerie stillness has draped the deck like a blanket, and an icy chill runs down my spine.

A man is wielding a gun. He's pointing it straight at the crowd. My heart stops, and my breath catches in my throat.

I scan the deck, but Dad is not where I last saw him. I don't see him anywhere. Fear courses through me like icy nails, freezing me in place. I know I should run, but where? A single gunshot slices through the air—I scream in sheer terror.

I am not the only one.

Everything happens so fast. I don't have time to run. I don't even have time to think. One shot evolves into many. Bullets whip through the air in all directions. The man turns and aims at me and instinctively, I hit the deck. My vision blurs, but not before I see drops of my blood splatter around me. Liquid heat blankets my skin and searing pain rips through my stomach. Then everything goes dark.

When I stir back to consciousness, the air is ringing with sirens and frantic screams. Burning pain radiates through my chest with every breath, and my pulse races, a reminder I'm still alive.

One thought thunders in my head: *find Dad.*

I push onto my elbows and survey the carnage around me. Bodies are strewn across the deck like broken dolls, some silent and still, others writhing in pain as fellow passengers scavenge their rations. The wood beneath them is drenched in blood, a river of red that covers the world in crimson.

I close my eyes for a moment and will the darkness to take me. I don't want to die like this, but I don't want to live this way either.

Someone tugs at the loaves of bread that I have gripped firmly, and my eyes snap open. A wild-eyed woman pries at my fingers, but I refuse to let go. "I have children."

"I am a child," I bellow, clutching the bread to my chest. The woman turns and walks away without a word. Just once she looks back, for what I don't know—I assume to see if I'm dead yet.

I give her the finger. That's when I see him wading through the sea of people, shouting my name. He doesn't stop until he's reached me. Relief is evident in his eyes, but they widen when he sees the scarlet stains on my shirt.

Dad pulls me into his arms and whispers words of comfort. For a moment, all I feel is relief—relief that we are both alive.

He looks into my eyes and smiles softly, "Abby, it'll be all right."

"My stomach—"

He reaches down and peels the blood-soaked shirt away from my skin. "It's not that bad," he says, after exhaling a heavy breath. "You're gonna be fine."

I nod. And stupidly, I believe him.

READ MORE:

https://books2read.com/thesickness

Made in the USA
Thornton, CO
04/15/24 21:02:53

30d6984f-f357-4f22-892a-53f701fb3660R01